D1212088

Bubbeh

Bubbeh

by
Sabina Berman

translated from the Spanish by
Andrea G. Labinger

LATIN AMERICAN LITERARY REVIEW PRESS
SERIES: DISCOVERIES
1998

The Latin American Literary Review Press publishes Latin American
creative writing under the series title Discoveries,
and critical works under the series title Explorations.

No part of this book may be reproduced by any means, including
information storage and retrieval or photocopying, except for short excerpts
quoted in critical articles, without written permission of the publisher.

Copyright © 1998 Latin American Literary Review Press

Library of Congress Cataloging-in-Publication Data:

Berman, Sabina.
    [Bobe. English]
    Bubbeh / by Sabina Berman ; translated from the Spanish by
Andrea G. Labinger.
        p.   cm. -- (Series Discoveries)
    ISBN 0-935480-93-5
    I. Labinger, Andrea G.   II. Title.   III. Series: Discoveries.
PQ7298. 12. E68B6313 1998
863--dc21   98-5560
                                                                      CIP

The paper used in this publication meets the minimum requirements of the
American National Standard for Permanence of Paper for Printed Library
Materials Z39.48-1984.∞

Latin American Literary Review Press
121 Edgewood Avenue
Pittsburgh, PA 15218

*M*y grandmother died tidily. I think that she died from an excess of tidiness. I don't know, that's the idea I had when I was a girl and it just stayed with me. In any event, it's better than saying she died of a cerebral embolism. Nobody dies from that: embolisms are the outcome of gradual deterioration, a drop spilled from a glass, literally a drop or trickle of blood that spills into the brain and blots it out. I can imagine my grandmother at the moment of her death:

She's lying in the bathtub, her body smaller than the length of the tub; she's thinking: "Blessed art Thou, Lord our God, King of the Universe." It's a white moment: she's very pale, her skin is the color of milk. She's so thin that her white knees are the widest part of her short, skinny legs. Looking down at her ankles you see the green veins, the blue arteries (that network of veins and arteries that I used to stare at when she took me to the *mikvah*); her thin body, seen through the nearly still water, seems to float. The tub is white, the water looks white, the tiled walls are white; suspended above the fog of the room, the overhead lightbulb is so yellow that it's almost white. My grandmother's hair is white, but her eyes are black, dark eyes on either side of that short, hooked nose: nose of a Sephardic Jew. Then she closes her eyes, the only blackness is extinguished, and in her mind—now a blank—these words are repeated, one after another: "Blessed art Thou, Lord our God, King of the Universe." And then everything goes red. It's the drop of blood that spills over her pristine thoughts.

I don't know, as I told you, these were the ideas of a little girl.

When I first knew her she was a tall woman, just as all adults are tall, and she was always very fastidious. My first memory of being with her was when she took me to the zoo. I'm holding her white-gloved hand. She shows me the giraffe pavilion. But I see only her: she's wearing a very delicate veil over her eyes, a little beige hat. She is the most elegant woman in the world. Through her veil, as through a lattice, I look at the giraffes. Their necks raised to the sky, they advance with identical movements to the drinking trough that's affixed to the highest part of the stone wall, their rhythms coinciding.

She says something to me in her strange, extravagantly accented Spanish, with her slow, measured voice. Her voice slips from Spanish into Yiddish. She's asking: "How do you say *giraffe* in Spanish?" I speak Yiddish because she taught me. It's been about ten years since I've had a conversation in Yiddish. It's been almost twenty-nine since I realized that this language of old European Jewry, this archaic form of German, born at the beginning of the second millennium, fermented in medieval ghettoes, mixed with Hebrew, Romance and Saxon languages wouldn't do me any good at all except to speak with my grandmother and the Yiddish teachers who taught me later on in elementary school, or perhaps to astonish someone by saying suddenly: "Oh, well, yes, I do speak Yiddish," an affirmation that seems not to cause too much of a stir in most cases. At any rate, I speak Yiddish. Yiddish resides in a particular part of my memory. In that same zone, my grandmother whispers into my ear: *szirafen*, giraffes in Yiddish, and just then, a giraffe arrogantly and deliberately dips its snout into the water dish.

"*Ber*," she says, kneeling before me. "*Ber*," pressing her lips together to form the *b*.

"*Oso*," I say in Spanish, and out of the corner of my eye, I see a large, fat monkey with long white fur climb up a pile of white rocks towards the white clouds.

"*Oso*," I whisper into grandmother's ear. She thinks it over, then repeats somewhat curiously: "*Oso*."

At midnight a humming noise awakens me, a sea-sound. I'm in that big bed. I've sunk into the fluffy mattress, under the absurdly thick coverlet. My perspiring head is on an enormous goose-feather pillow. The sea-sound continues, deliberately. I turn my head.

On the nightstand, under the extinguished lamp, there's a glass. Something floats in this glass: teeth, dentures. There's another glass next to it, containing another, smaller set of dentures. The glasses sit on top of a book. Also sitting on top of the book, at the base of the glasses, is something else, something shiny. A row of...of teeth? No, not teeth. Pearls, gray pearls. There are peeling gold letters on the dark spine of the leather-bound book. I don't recognize these letters. In kindergarten they don't teach these letters. Maybe there are many more letters than the ones they teach me. Maybe I'm dreaming, because the sea-noise is growing louder. I must be in a berth on a boat, floating on a black ocean. I can feel the swell. I sense the gentle rocking of the boat in the rocking of the bed next to mine.

In that bed next, a white lump is sleeping. It's a big, fat lump; it inflates and deflates. A bear. It's growling, snoring; that must be the sea-noise. No: there are two growls that I'm hearing, rhythmic growls, sometimes followed by a long whistle. Then a creak. The bed is creaking and rocking under the weight of the lump.

The lump rolls around a little. I see two heads peeking out from under the covers. They are outlined in the darkness: my grandmother's face and the face of a bear. My grandmother, hugged by a bear. It's a tame bear: it sniffs her face and runs its tongue over her cheek. It's a momentary vision, because then the lump rolls over again and I can see it only as something under the covers that inflates and deflates, growling and whistling like the distant sea.

Farther away, the bright curtains. Farther still, the yellow, yellow lights of the street lamps, their bulbs reaching as high as the terrace.

In their respective glasses, the dentures swim side by side like two fish in twin fishbowls. Beneath my cheek, my fevered sweat on the pillow.

My grandfather sits at the head of the table in his shirtsleeves with his glasses perched at the end of his bulbous nose. He's reading a book. The table is set for ten with a white lace tablecloth. At family reunions it can be extended another yard. I sit at the opposite end: grandfather needs complete silence when he studies. I'm sitting on a cushion so that my eyes are at table level. From time to time I spear a piece of herring with my fork and I nibble at it. Then I take a drink from my water glass.

Grandfather reaches out for the newspaper at his side. He puts it on top of his book. He clenches his teeth. I know this morning ritual, and I love the part where he reads the newspaper. As he turns the page, his face reddens. He squeezes his right hand into a fist. He starts to sputter, shaking his head. There's something wrong with the newspaper, with the world. "Shit," he says under his breath.

He laughs to himself, but it's a horrible kind of laugh. He tightens his jaw again. Grandmother returns from the kitchen with the tea-tray. Little white porcelain cups with a cobalt blue border, silver teapot and sugar bowl.

She places the tray on the corner of the table where my grandfather continues his lament, and she pours out the tea into three cups. Angrily, grandfather barks something out at her in Yiddish. My grandmother covers one eye with her hand and cries, "*Oy-oy-oy.*" That's how she complains: "*Oy-oy-oy.*"

Plaintively, she closes his newspaper; he is talking loudly and pawing at the air. My grandmother takes the newspaper into the kitchen to throw it away. Grandfather's shouts follow her in three languages: Yiddish, Polish and Spanish. Those damned Russians, those communists, those gringos—they're all Nazis. Damned bureaucrats, damned Mexicans, to hell with those Arabs, damned stupid Jews. Lousy politician bastards. The victims of his rage may change, but his rage is eternal.

He reads the book again. It's always the same thing. A book made of parchment paper and tiny Hebrew letters. Maimonides's *Guide for the Perplexed*. Years later I will learn that this is a book to be read at breakfast. He calms down, concentrates, rocks in his chair and says: "Hmm, ah, hmm." Behind him there's an oil painting of four sunflowers in a clay vase, all done in ochres and yellows.

My grandmother takes the silver tongs and deposits a cube of sugar in one cup. Another. Another. A fourth cube. She puts the sweetened tea next to the book.

The Aizbergs are dangerous people. As we near the midpoint of our journey in the lovely yellow streetcar, my heart skips as I realize we're approaching where they live. They live downtown; we take a taxi to a run-down building.

I climb the stairs holding my grandmother's gloved hand. I observe the overlapping, peeling layers of paint on the walls. I know, because Mr. Aizberg once told me, that from the moment we ring the bell until we reach their fifth-floor apartment, he will be hunting for his pants and his shirt in the closet, putting them on, and his wife will be turning on the lights that are hidden in the corners of the dark, windowless room. It's just that they have to economize; if Mr. Aizberg sat around in his pants and shirt, they would wear out at the elbows and knees, rubbing against the furniture, and since they have to save on electricity, their eyes have become accustomed to the darkness.

The door opens halfway, and Mr. Aizberg's balding head peeks out. He admits us to a dark space whose corners are dimly lit by little lamps with grayish shades. The sofas shine. Their plastic slipcovers glisten like a layer of ice. It smells musty.

I want to leave, but we sit down on the sofa. Mr. Aizberg sits on the edge of a stool.

We hear footsteps approaching. Mrs. Aizberg hurries in from the hallway with anguished little steps. She has wavy white hair; she greets us in Yiddish with her plain-tive voice, as though the devil were chasing her and she were pleading for help with her dying breath.

I don't understand the conversation in Polish, but I sense the extent of the fear in their voices. My grandmother, on the other hand, seems impassive: she smiles, removes the glove from her right hand with her customary calm elegance, and clasps it in her other gloved hand.

At times Mr. Aizberg addresses me directly. On those occasions he speaks to me in broken Spanish, very simple words sprinkled with the detritus of other languages.

"Ve used to be called Aizenberg," he tells me. "Vit an *n*. Aizenberg. Pretty, no? Ve had a big house, *grosse*, trees, children, like you, *kinder*, eight children. Your *bubbeh* knew us back in Poland, esk her. Your *zayde* had the first car ever in Galizia. A model-T Ford. Ve had evertink, evertink. I could read, study, wery nice. Not work, no misery. I svear, evertink ve had. And the war came. And den nuttink. Evertink ve lost. Vhen ve got to Mexico, dey took away the last tink: the *n*. The police don't understand Aizenberg, never hear of Aizenberg. But maybe dey hear of ice mountains in the ocean: iceberg. So dat's vat dey put down: Aizberg. And my *neshome*, my soul, you know? Aizberg!"

I don't answer; I've heard this story ten, maybe thirty times before. I curl up on the sofa, raise my shoulders and let my chin fall on my chest. I really want to get out of here. I hear the far-off voices speaking Polish. I squint my eyes, trying to distinguish the books on the shelves that cover all the walls. Dark-spined books. If I close my eyes a little more, I can make out the gilded Hebrew letters on their spines, like golden sparks floating in the blackness. Polish, that harsh-ridged language, reverberates around me.

Sooner or later old Mr. Aizberg apologizes because they have no cake or cookies. They can offer us only tea. Sometimes he tells us there's no more tea either, and my grandmother replies that hot water is just fine, that plain hot water is wonderful for your health. Then he serves us glasses of hot water or bitter tea.

And sooner or later, always later as far as I'm concerned, there's the business about the doll. Mrs. Aizberg jumps up and runs with her mincing steps into the hallway. She returns with a very large doll, and she bends over to hand it to me. I take it. Something in my heart comes loose. She always gives me lovely dolls with perfect, round little faces and rosy cheeks. Brightly colored dresses. They're even wearing underwear beneath their dresses, sometimes made of lace. With eyes that open or close depending on whether you lift the doll up or lay it down.

Mrs. Aizberg still leans over me as I observe the details of the doll, wanting to capture my slightest reaction.

"I luff you wery much," she says, finally. She repeats: "I luff you wery much."

She goes to sit down in a chair, folding her hands in her lap without ever taking her eyes off me.

"I luff you wery much," she says again.

Her voice sounds exasperated, hungry, as though she's begging me for something: give me that, I don't know what, as she repeats over and over: "I luff you wery much."

My grandmother and Mr. Aizberg don't interfere; they let the scene continue between her and me. The woman bites her lip, and then says very quietly: "I luff you wery much."

It makes me want to cry. Sometimes I actually do burst into tears without really understanding why. I clutch the doll to my chest: Thank you. Thank you, thank you.

Dying of fright, I say: "Thank you very much. Let's go home now."

There is a little table next to the front door: my grandmother leaves a gold coin on it. She takes my hand in her gloved hand.

On the corner of that block is Piccolo, an ice cream place. Seated at one of the tables, my grandmother and I eat our ice cream. One day I ask her why we have to visit the Aizbergs.

"I don't like to go," I say.

My grandmother wipes her lips with the edge of her napkin. She tells me that no one likes to visit them, that's why we have to do it.

I console myself with a spoonful of ice cream.

With one upraised arm I hold my grandmother's white hand, while in the other I clutch the tiny hand of my doll. The doll flies down the street with her little arm raised. On the sidewalk the uneasy pigeons move throughout the Zócalo with the rhythm of a secondhand. My grandmother's profile is outlined against that of the cathedral: I see the golden clock atop the cathedral. My grandmother's profile comes forward, obscuring it.

The memory comes upon me suddenly. I'm running through my parents' house, running crazily down the long corridor clutching a big bag of pork rinds. My white patent leather shoes click down the steps to the darkness of the basement.

I'm in my bedroom when my grandmother comes in and leans down towards me, her arms spread wide. Her surprise visits fill me with joy, and I move forward into her embrace, but a sudden mental flash brings me these realizations: I have a bag of pork rinds in my hand, a pork rind in my mouth. From the time of Moses, God has forbidden us to eat pork; I am in mortal sin. But that's not the worst part: the worst part is that she, my grandmother, the holiest woman in the universe, might ask me for a piece of whatever I'm eating, and then, what will I do? Do I admit that I'm a sinner and make her suffer, or do I give her a pork rind without telling her that it's pork and let her suffer damnation on my account? It's an intolerable situation, so I escape her hug and run out of the bedroom. She follows me, asking why I'm avoiding her: "*Mein kind, far vos*?" Why, darling? No matter what, I'm making her unhappy, so I go into the kitchen that's redolent of chicken and go out again. I cross into the living room where my brother Jorge is playing monotonous scales on the piano. I go down to the basement and push open the door into the gleaming realm where the washing machine groans.

When my grandmother catches up with me, I'm compulsively trampling on the bag of pork rinds. Then the washer stops, and in the silence of that light-filled room, my grandmother stares at me from her cathedral height, her eyes enormous.

"Hi," I say to her. "Hi, I'm crazy."

I'm going to the psychoanalyst with my mother. Sometimes she goes alone, and sometimes I go along with her. Sometimes we also go to the dentist together. Going to the psychoanalyst is much better. But going to the hairdresser is the best. Actually we don't go to the psychoanalyst very often. We sit down in the waiting room, each in our own armchair. We look at magazines or else I spread my notebooks out on my lap and I write.

The psychoanalyst's name is Santiago. He wears short-sleeved shirts and wide pants; he has lots of curly hair, sprinkled with gray, and his face has Indian features. His black eyes look huge through his Coke-bottle glasses. He comes out to greet us and he tweaks my nose. My mother and I go into the inner office.

She told him about the day when my grandmother stopped being tall.

My mother came out of the office with wet eyes and a sense of urgency. She grabbed my hand and while we were walking she said, "Forget about swimming class. We've got to talk to *Bubbeh*."

It's very simple, really: my mother wants to know if the doll she had when she was a little girl ended up in the trash. She asks my grandmother this question in an aggrieved tone.

My grandmother observes her.

"That was twenty-five years ago," she says quietly.

They're standing in the middle of the living room, talking. I seem to remember them talking in Yiddish, although my mother switches over to Spanish in the middle of her sentences.

Mother demands to know the truth about the doll. The doll had broken in two, right across its chest, and my grandmother put the pieces in a shoebox and mailed it to a doll hospital in the Swiss Alps, where the doll met an English prince who gave up his throne to marry the doll, a commoner. They moved to Dubrovnik, by the ocean.

My grandmother smiles.

"Well, it wasn't exactly like that," she concedes.

My mother is distraught, trying to make herself understood.

The doll isn't the important thing here; what's important is that my grandmother didn't allow her to mourn its death. It's just that my grandmother never allowed her to cry. That she always hid sadness from her.

That's why she still can't cry, even now. That's why her crisis now, at age thirty, is interminable.

My grandmother sends me to the study. There, among Mrs. Aizberg's dolls, I need to choose the prettiest one and bring it to my mother.

In the study, I kneel down behind the green corduroy armchair. I open the door of the bookcase. On the next-to-the-last shelf: twenty dolls. The Dutch girl, the doll from Tehuantepec, the Scottish soldier with a bagpipe, Queen Victoria in her pale green velvet dress trimmed with gold, with her white wig and ruby-studded tiara. The little Black doll dressed in a tiger-skin loincloth. I scrutinize them one by one. I choose the Black doll.

But I recall the feeling: I find myself in the dark, because a thunderclap has put out the electricity, intermittently illuminating and then obscuring the yellow walls in the pauses between the thunderbolts. Through the window I see the sky rending itself out in sheets of rain. I feel my abandonment without my mother at my side, the total abandonment when I recognize that the storm is raging inside her. This storm within my mother, that calms itself for days at a time and suddenly bursts forth again: this is her crisis at age thirty. To appease her I must find a more valuable offering than the Black doll, a greater sacrifice. Repentant, I grab Queen Victoria.

It's useless. When I return to the living room with Queen Victoria in my arms, my mother is no longer discussing dolls.

Why didn't my grandmother tell her that my grandfather was unfaithful, that he had other women? It would have saved my mother years of expensive psychoanalysis. Why, when they fled Poland just before the Nazi invasion, didn't she explain to her that the Jews were considered a cursed race that should be exterminated from the planet? Why did she tell her that other ridiculous story: that God led the Jews out of Poland, just as he had led them from Egypt many years before, to a better, a safer country?

No thanks to my grandmother, my mother grew up with a fairy-tale mentality until her own children were born and she started psychoanalysis, overcome by a reality that by no means could be considered enchanted.

For a while now my grandmother pretends not to listen to my mother. She's looking out the bay window at the sky. My mother gets up from the sofa and passes by her to go into the kitchen.

Halfway there, she sees me. She sees Queen Victoria in my arms. She smiles at me and says something horrible: "Dolls don't exist." And she continues on to the kitchen.

In one split second the small cataclysm occurred: my grandmother looks towards the bay window, now brightened by sunshine; my mother gets up from the sofa and passes by her side. I realize that my mother is a head taller than she is.

Alone, a silhouette in the brightness of the living room, Grandmother begins to hum a little song to herself, bending her head slowly first towards one shoulder, then the other. My *bubbeh* is so small, so small.

She raises the palm of her hand to her cheek and continues shaking her head, singing gently: "*Oy bai boi, oy bay bei bai boi…*"

Even now it still seems quite a feat to me that my grandmother told my mother about the escape from the Nazis as though it were a holy pilgrimage. I think about my grandfather turning the keys to his brush factory over to the production engineer, handing over the keys to their house in Bielsko-Biala to a servant boy. I think about my grandfather, my grandmother, their children, walking through the snow behind the ox-cart that carried the few belongings they were allowed to keep; I think about them sleeping in stables, in cellars, riding in crammed trains along with other people with desperate faces and opaque eyes. I think of them under an ancient tree, spread out against a sky where distant planes whistle by like little black crosses against a navy blue background, and the sudden bombs, and then all of them suddenly falling to the ground, covered in dirty snow. There they are, riding the Trans-Siberian train, six people locked up in a cabin for days and days, the penetrating cold, hunger, my grandfather and grandmother and their children marching through Moscow, by then a nearly abandoned city, a gray city where people scurry by, eyes on the asphalt, fleeing, a place where no one dares to stop for more than a minute to speak to strangers. There they are, peeking into a bakery window, displaying dainty plaster breads. Then back on the train, finally en route to Tokyo with their worn clothing and no passports. My uncle, standing in the lobby of an Asian luxury hotel, quietly standing, watching the measured movements of the distinguished guests and the bellhops in livery, knowing that the family can't sit on the furniture, that if their worn-out pants were to graze the yellow silk of that sofa over there, it would cause a scandal. There's my grandfather, begging on a street corner; my grandmother, in the Japanese dentist's office, having him remove a diamond filling that she hurriedly had concealed in a rear molar. There they are again, on a Japanese ship bound for America, the land of liberty, of opportunity, heroic cradle of democracy. Now they're seated at the table of Princess Hikari, a teenage princess, no more than a girl, lost in the copious folds of a red kimono which is embroidered with golden clouds. Her face is mask-white, but frozen into a sweet expression. Piled against the walls of the stateroom are the boxes containing the princess's dowry, destined along with her for a rich Japanese businessman from San Francisco. Although they've never seen one another, it's the most suitable marriage possible. Now my grandfather leaps from his bed, peering through the porthole at the rolling, rolling sea, and Japan has finally entered the war in alliance with Germany and Italy, as everyone had anticipated, and the ship returns to the nightmare world from which they had hoped to escape. My grandfather, his wife and children, the other refugees are all toasting each other with *sake*, because it's really just a round-trip cruise, a ritual to honor the princess who has thrown herself overboard, committing suicide. Unable to submit to the embrace of a stranger and to life in a barbaric country, she dressed herself in a sky-blue kimono with embroidered multicolored butterflies and gave herself to the black, midnight sea. There's my grandfather, reading the telegram that denies them entry into San Francisco, the coast of the land of liberty, of opportunity, the heroic cradle of democracy in plain sight, while in the bow of the ship, my grandfather, surrounded by his family, reads the telegram aloud. They disembark in the wrong place, in Manzanillo, on the coast of Mexico, a country to which only a single fact connects them: there, in the past century, the blond Duke Maximilian, nephew of Emperor Franz Josef of the Austro-Hungarian Empire, after a well-meaning, but clumsy, unpopular and ultimately brief reign, had been shot on orders of an indigenous gentleman, a certain Benito Juárez. This admirable detail, that secretly linked the fate of reviled Jews with that of an unknown Indian, not only obliterated the notion of superior races (the European), but also spilled the blood of one of its most aristocratic representatives. There's my grandfather, gluing the bristles of a brush to a wooden handle and sealing his creation in the oven of their tiny kitchen; grandfather selling brushes in a corner of the Zócalo in Mexico City; Grandmother clutching the hands of her son and daughter, deliberately getting lost in the tangle of aisles of the immense La Merced market among the odors of fruit, fish, butter, cheese and chiles; the rabbi blessing the first brush-making machine that would later be the beginning of the Glickman Company's factory.

These are images that I collected as a girl, plucked from here and there in my uncles' houses, from my parents, with the same determination that inspires other children to collect stickers or my brother to collect postage stamps. Just as the stamps gave my brother a vague idea of the breadth of the world, these memories have done the same for me. These few images: it will take me years to sort them out and decipher them, and even after all that, they will always seem insufficient to me. I don't know, perhaps the past can only be a scarcity of images. Among all of them, of course, the one that shines with a special light is that of the diamond encrusted into the molar at the back of my grandmother's mouth.

That's what my grandmother is to me: the woman who has her wisdom tooth excavated to store a diamond, and then, when the last resources have been exhausted and no one knows how to keep on going, she removes the diamond and asks: "Will this do?"

I speak to my mother about this man called Moses. We're in the dining room; my brothers have gone out into the garden to play. I tell her that Moses, infused with God's strength, opened his arms and the Red Sea parted, and then, followed by the Jewish people, he advanced between the walls of the risen sea.

My mother listens, amused, her green-gray eyes turning turquoise, as they do when she's happy. When I finish my story, she brushes a blonde curl from her forehead and explains:

"This guy Moses was an Egyptian astronomer who understood the tides and arrived at the Red Sea just when the water level was very low. Besides, the Red Sea wasn't a sea at all, it was a lake with very calm waters. And it wasn't really red. So it's like this: Moses arrived at exactly the right moment when he could cross that pond without any problems."

Then next day in Bible class, I raise my hand. I say: "Moses was an Egyptian who studied astronomy..."

The teacher interrupts me and corrects me: "Moses was a Jew."

"No," I insist. "He was an Egyptian who told lies to the Jews; he told them he was Jewish."

"Wait for me in the office," the teacher says.

In school they teach me things that I have to un-learn at home. They teach me things at home, and I'm ex-pelled from school.

My mother explains: "The business about the Jews being God's chosen people is what we call a miracle of the imagination. Look: we Jews are the most abused people in history. Every fifty or one hundred years some tyrant comes along and tries to exterminate us. Every time some country wants to blame someone for its problems, they blame the Jews, and we Jews, what do we do? We delude ourselves with the story that God, that invisible guy, that hypotheti-cal gentleman (later we'll discuss the meaning of *hypo-thetical*), really adores us. You see? Sheer craziness."

The next day I come home with an expulsion no-tice.

Because in those days my mother was studying to become a psychoanalyst and she worked in the insane asy-lum every morning, she sent me to my grandmother's for the time I was expelled from school. I would arrive at my grandmother's house with tales of my martyrdom. No one was fair, no one understood my feelings. Grandmother lis-tened to me, sighing.

"Well," she said, "that's life. There are thirty-six wise and just people in the world. And those thirty-six *tzadikim* hold up the whole universe with all its stars."

It was no great consolation to hear this, because my grandmother couldn't tell me where those few holy people lived. Even worse, it seemed that each one of them lived in a different part of the world, and the people around them didn't know how holy they were. Because they were so discreet, so anonymous, some of the *tzadikim* didn't even know themselves that they were among the thirty-six pil-lars of the universe.

"Only thirty-six," I would say to myself, thoughtfully.

That meant, if my childlike calculations were cor-rect, the vast majority of people whom I knew and who knew me, as well as those whom I would know for the rest

of my life, were unfair and foolish. At least in this one pes-
simistic way of looking at the world, my mother and grandmother agreed.

I remember the afternoon I arrived at my
grandmother's house bearing the story of Moses, the Egyptian astronomer. My grandmother opened her eyes very
wide and without letting me finish, she assured me that my
mother was doing the right thing by going to the insane
asylum every morning, because it was obvious that she had
been a little nervous lately, and of course Moses had parted
the Red Sea in the name of God and with the strength of
the Lord our God, King of the Universe.

It was different when I talked with her directly about
God. My grandmother would wash the dishes after lunch,
and I would explain to her what *hypothetical* meant.

"So God is an idea that makes us feel less alone."

My grandmother dropped the plate she was washing right into the sink. Sadly, she fished out each piece of
china one by one. She started to put the plate back together
on top of the stove without even looking at me. Arching
and lowering her eyebrows, furrowing her brow, she was
clearly thinking very hard.

I kept on talking, enchanted with my own wisdom.
I opened the refrigerator and took out a bunch of purple
grapes. While I popped grape after grape into my mouth, I
kept on explaining about *God the Hypothetical*. I told her
how I had visited a church with my mother. The parishio-
ners were praying, and every so often the priest, next to the
golden altar, would mention God's name. Then everyone
would say *Amen*. My mother had asked me if I could see
the God they were talking about, and Whom the Father
kept mentioning; and since I couldn't, since He was invisible, then if I could hear whether God answered the parish-
ioners with words or with some kind of sign, a creaking
pew, maybe, or a change in the Virgin's expression. I had
watched the Virgin for a full half-hour, watched the congregation, the pews.

"No, God doesn't answer," I said. "And they keep on calling His name anyway," my mother pointed out. "That's what you call faith."

I continued eating grapes and talking, mocking the congregation and their *Amens*, while laughing with amusement at my own cleverness, all with the same mouth, a mouth that was very big indeed that day. And my grandmother, absorbed in her own thoughts, continued putting the pieces of the broken plate together.

Suddenly I felt sad. I stopped talking. The water continued running out of the tap into the sink.

Finally my grandmother said: "Close your eyes." I squeezed my lids shut.

"What do you see?"

"Nothing."

"And in that nothing, do you see a light?"

I concentrated. Beneath my eyelids in that darkness something like a yellow and white dust shimmered, a light.

"Yes," I said. "But I always see that."

"Always?"

I thought. That light didn't seem extraordinary in any way.

"Yes," I said, "always."

"Always," my grandmother repeated. "Well, that light is God, and it has many names."

One afternoon I asked my grandmother what the war had really been like. She went to the kitchen to check on the chicken soup, and I followed her.

"Tell me what it feels like to be in a war."

She went to the balcony to pour water into the flowerpots.

"My mother remembers something like a wave of snow, and my uncle remembers a yellow sofa."

My grandmother put her index finger up to her ear.

"Listen to the water in the earth, glug, glug, glug."

It was difficult to hear the water gurgling in the flow-erpots: the din of the traffic seven stories below was louder.

"Water," she said, "water." "Water," she repeated, behind the green fan of a potted palm.

"They're going to flunk me in school because of all of you," I said. "They just tell me things fast, like they re-ally don't want to tell them at all, and they tell me every-thing without any feeling. Besides, I know that they're hid-ing the things about...How do you say it? The things about..."

I clenched my fists. My grandmother was watching me.

"Tell me about when you escaped through Russia," I said.

My grandmother went to the wardrobe to take out a sheet, and I followed. Finally she sat down on the edge of the bed.

"All right," she said. "I'm going to tell you the most exciting part of the trip."

I sat down by her side, expectantly.

My mind was filled with black uniforms, with the SS, gray uniforms, with Soviet soldiers, with bombs fall-ing on either side of the train, with the bloodstained snow and pieces of bodies scattered in the red snow. They were images taken from books, from the Holocaust movie they showed every month in school, from magazines. Besides the war documentaries they showed us, I supplemented them with more: films I had seen on television, sensation-alistic books I had read, a sinister, mocking pamphlet pub-lished by some neo-Nazis from the Santa María de la Rivera neighborhood. Once you breach the boundaries of horror, it can become addictive. I ran my tongue over my lips, tast-ing the bitterness in anticipation.

My grandmother had her eyes closed. With her first words she opened them again.

"We're on the train," she says slowly, as if each word is an effort. "Your mommy is next to me, and I'm next to the window. Your grandpa is opposite us, sleeping. Next to him your uncle is sleeping."

"Yes," I say.

"Yes," says my *bubbeh*. "It's early morning. I open the window and the cold air comes in."

"It's snowing out," I say.

"No, the fields are green, very green. Winter has just ended. And out there in the green field, far away, there are three white cows. Three fat cows, grazing. Like three little snowballs. And I take out my handkerchief and wave it through the window and I tell them good-bye, good-bye."

Here my grandmother smiles and sighs. She goes on: "And your mommy," she says, "who is about your age, but she's very blonde and she has long braids and a skinny little face…"

"That's because she's hungry," I say.

"Your mommy," my grandmother says, ignoring my interruption, "your mommy, with her little hand…yes, with her little hand, she says to the cows, good-bye, good-bye."

A moment passes. Grandmother repeats: "Good-bye."

"Yes," I say, "but what about the Nazis and the bombs and all the dead people?"

She watches me.

"Bring me the blue lotion from the bathroom," she says, finally. And she stands up to spread the white sheet out against the air with a single movement.

She puts lotion on the freshly-washed sheets, my grandmother does.

I'm in the big bed, as fluffy as a cloud. A long, white bed. My grandmother covers me up to my chin with the goose-down comforter, and she sits down on the edge of the bed. The bedroom is in shadows.

My grandmother leans over to peer into my eyes. It's an ageless moment. I'm eight years old, perhaps six or even four. Once more my grandmother becomes that tall woman whose profile extends upward, covering the cathedral's golden clock. Her black eyes penetrating my eyes. Her face, as white as the moon's reflection in a pond. The pond, my face, illuminated by her own. She passes her hand from my forehead down to my cheeks, half-closing my eyelids.

Her measured voice, distant and close at the same time: "Do you see that light?"

With her index and ring fingers, she taps the comforter on my chest. I hardly feel the pressure.

Yes, that greenish-white light, inside me.

"*Ayn sof*," she says, scarcely breathing the words.

Everything is like a secret. What my grandmother is now entrusting to me is, in fact, a secret.

"*Ayn sof*," I reply very quietly.

Years later I will learn that *Ayn sof* means *without end* in Hebrew. It will take me even longer to fully comprehend that this is one of the names of God. I will be astonished at the simplicity with which my grandmother has asked me if I see that light and at the ingenuousness with which I answer simply, *yes*.

How that light can be the foundation of all possible experience, how that amorphous stuff can solidify itself into the incalculable profusion of existing forms, how Everything can be made of such fragile, ephemeral material—such enormous questions could not fit or even begin to take root in my childlike brain. From adolescence onward, though, they will begin to obsess me. I will turn away from them, only to return in unexpected ways. I will withdraw yet again, overcome by the vastness of these issues and the subtlety of their essence: that light.

I write this slowly, timidly. I feel the hesitation of someone who opens a forbidden door, of someone who gives the keys to a personal treasure-chest to the third stranger she passes in the street.

It's white and green and simple, so simple. That light. I have closed my eyelids on it. Between my eyes I feel my grandmother's kiss.

My grandfather steps out of his gray Valiant, crosses over to the flower stand against the wall at the end of the block, and picks out a bouquet of roses. A big bouquet of red roses. I can see him from the balcony of the apartment. I go over to the sofa and sit down, listening to my grandmother bustling about in the kitchen. With delighted expectancy I wait, as if the roses were for me.

But my grandfather never shows up. Soon my mother arrives, without flowers, to pick me up and take me home.

I rummage through my grandfather's desk drawers. What am I looking for? It doesn't matter. What I find obliterates any possible motives for my search. It's a white pen with the figure of a woman running along its entire length. She's dressed entirely in black: a long, black dress, black gloves, luxuriant blonde hair. If I tip the pen a little, her gloves creep up her arms all the way to her shoulders and her skirt rides up to her knees. If I tip it a little more, she's standing there in just her black underwear and high-heeled shoes. If I lay it flat, she's naked and barefoot, standing on the tips of her little white toes like an unusually well-endowed ballerina.

It's a remarkable invention, but it's not mine, so I hide it underneath the papers where I found it and I shut the drawer.

How it showed up in my backpack at school the next day, I'll never know.

I stare at it exhaustively in Bible class, as I sit at my desk at the back of the room. The woman in her long black dress; the woman gradually undressed. It disturbs me. There is a mystery here that I must penetrate. With a little knife I use to sharpen pencils, I cut through the plastic film that covers the woman's portrait. Suddenly, she's completely naked and my fingers are covered with black ink.

The eternally naked blonde. Carefully, so that no one will see me, I throw the pen into the wastebasket.

Months go by. Then the news: my grandfather wants a divorce after forty years of marriage. He is going to live in a motel. The rabbi has told him that it's his right—as a man—to demand a divorce whenever he wants one, but he also says that it's difficult for him to understand why he of all people should consider it necessary at this point. My grandfather alleges that they are no longer sexually compatible. After forty years of marriage, this is what my grandfather says.

And how could they still be compatible, my mother asks, when he's been compatible with half the women in Mexico.

My uncle is standing in my mother's bedroom without proffering an opinion. He's wearing a navy blue silk suit, a sky blue silk shirt, a red silk tie, and little gold cufflinks bearing his initials, *M.G.*, in steel blue. Impeccable and silky as always, but scared shitless.

My mother, seated on one of the sectionals of the sofa, crosses one ankle over the other and stretches out her legs.

"Sit down," she says to my uncle.

He stares straight ahead at the empty spot on the sofa and sobs.

It's shameful, he says. He and his son will never be able to hold their heads up. So embarrassing. How could he not have known. At the factory, Grandfather always stares intently at anything in high heels. He's hired a new secretary who doesn't know how to type, who can't answer the phone properly, can't take dictation, and despite all that, he has her come into his office so he can read Goethe poems to her, translated into Spanish. Goethe, that anti-Semite, for God's sake. Excerpts from Goethe's *Faust*, the parts where the devil speaks of love. Where a devil, a *goy* devil— that's the worst part—speaks of love. "Marguerite, immortalize me with a glance," he tells the secretary. His son, my uncle, would gladly run to Siberia right this minute.

A case of delayed adolescence: My grandfather's office is in the same building as the machinery. It has smoked-glass windows, and from any angle of the factory you can see his silhouette chasing the secretary's. My uncle wipes his nose with the back of his hand.

And all of a sudden my grandfather stops at times and give a military salute to the presidential portrait that hangs on the wall. What a perverted sense of humor! All the workers smile when my grandfather does this. Just the other day at a meeting with the union leaders my grandfather made a suggestion to the workers. Although he said it very slowly, my uncle could have sworn he said it in Yiddish. "Besides making brushes, they could brush up against this," my grandfather said, grabbing his crotch.

"The earth should swallow me up," my uncle says.

"Sit down," my mother asks him again.

He continues staring at the empty spot on the sofa.

My uncle has stomach acid problems. Constantly. Yesterday the doctor diagnosed an incipient ulcer. His father's rejuvenation is killing him. Grandfather has begun growing a Stalinesque mustache. "It's coming out black— tell me, is that fair? Black, just like Stalin's...Age," my uncle says, "it only makes us worse."

From his jacket pocket he extracts a gold cigarette

case, engraved with his initials, *M.G.*, in Gothic script. He looks inside at the cigarettes.

"I shouldn't," he says, and snaps the case shut.

He says: "He swore to me that he'd at least shave off the mustache." And, after a long pause: "Vulgarity. There should be a vaccine against it…"

He leaves without saying good-bye, absorbed in his misery.

Later on I emerge from my mother's dressing room and find her reading a book. Without lifting her face she tells me that my uncle is afraid of getting lost.

"Getting lost?"

"Didn't you see all those initials?"

We've just entered my grandmother's house. My mother embraces her, cheek against cheek.

"Congratulations," she whispers, "you got rid of him."

She kisses her on one cheek and then the other. My mother is exultant. She drops her handbag on the sofa and turns around dramatically to sing a song in German. It must be a funny little song, because my grandmother's cheeks turn red and she responds with another little song in Yiddish. She sings it in her fine voice, keeping the beat with her hand. It sounds like a children's ditty with a simple refrain, but it strikes me as absurd nonetheless: a horse that gives orders to its rider, or something equally nonsensical. The ending is unforgettable. My *bubbeh* asks this question: "And what were their names? Schmuck and Schmuck!"

My grandmother, normally so pale, is suddenly all red. She presses her lips together. The *bad* word had burst forth unexpectedly from her lips, not once, but twice. Profoundly vexed, she stares into the distance, as if she didn't know what she was saying.

"Now you're finally finished with that business about the children," my mother says, as she pulls a chair over from the table and sits down.

"The last one has left home," she says. She tells her that my uncle is meeting with my grandfather at the rabbi's house to calculate a monthly allowance for my grandmother. It should be enough to let her keep the apartment with some money left over for travel. Now, finally, my grandmother can begin to lead a civilized existence. The first place, of course, should be Paris. How long has it been since my grandmother has seen Paris?

My grandmother interrupts in Polish, but my mother cuts her short.

"If he wants a harem," she says, "let him behave like a sultan."

Bubbeh doesn't want me to listen anymore. She's already heard enough, she says, and begs my mother to speak in Polish.

"No, let her listen, so she'll know."

My mother takes her in her arms, she dances. Suddenly, my grandmother, no longer able to resist, lets herself dance. She throws her head backward like a young girl swept away by the beauty of the dance.

They dance through the room, a waltz without music. *Bubbeh* holds out her hand to me, and the three of us are dancing.

The walls whirl slowly around us, the gauze curtains disappearing and reappearing, puffed up with air and light.

Walking around with an air of calm, my mother enumerates various destinations for my grandmother's trip. With great pleasure she names a city, then lets it solidify in silence, while she keeps pacing and dreaming of foreign streets that my grandmother and I imagine her imagining as she walks between the sofa and the dining room table, now watching her straight hair glint golden as she approaches the inflating and deflating window curtains, now watching it turn dark as she approaches us. New York, Brussels, Brugge. Ah, Brugge. Paris.

We hear a key turn in the door. The door opens.

There stands my grandfather, his grouchy face framed by the upturned collar of his overcoat and the droopy brim of his hat. With two suitcases. My mother falls back into the armchair, and my grandmother gets up from the sofa. Then nobody moves.

Finally my grandmother asks my grandfather if he wants a cup of tea.

"Yes," my grandfather says, and puts the suitcases down on the floor.

My grandmother returns from the kitchen with the tea-tray, the delicate little white porcelain cups with their cobalt blue border, the silver English teapot, the silver sugar bowl. She places the tray on the table, which is covered with a lace tablecloth. My grandfather still stands there between his two suitcases with his hat and his overcoat, but with an expressionless face.

My grandmother serves four cups of tea.

I don't want any tea. It tastes like nothing to me. My mother doesn't want any, either. She has a killer stomachache. That's what she says, *killer*.

With the silver tongs, my *bubbeh* places four lumps of sugar in a cup.

"*Kim*," she tells my grandfather, "come."

In a serious voice, he says that the rabbi sends his regards.

I see them sitting at the table, lifting their little cups, looking into each other's eyes. Lowering the little cups, still looking into one another's eyes. The steam from the tea. The fragrance.

I see them as I never saw them before and never would again, looking into each other's eyes.

My mother says that she married a man who was extremely handsome, extremely competent professionally, extremely conceited and treacherous—a womanizer, an absent father, and other such atrocities. She says all this because my grandmother married a man who was stamped from exactly the same mold. That's the only explanation for the fact that my mother, an otherwise intelligent and sensible woman, could have fallen into the clutches of such a specimen.

My grandmother lifts her cup of tea; with her other hand she lifts the saucer. She lowers the saucer into her lap and replaces the cup.

My mother says that my grandmother didn't teach her to have dignity, that she never taught her to express her own desires, that in the presence of men my grandmother is silent and eternally obliging. My mother recognizes how terrible this is, since she has been the same way. In the company of men she, too, has canceled herself out, and this is a terrible feeling, this shame for existing, this self-loathing. But anyway, enough is enough.

"Enough!" my mother shouts.

My grandmother stares into her cup.

"Well, all right," my mother says, as she continues pacing around the living room. After all, my grandmother belongs to a long line of such women: they cook and keep silent, they put flowers in vases, they braid their daughters' hair, they teach the children songs while they polish their shoes, they make the furniture gleam, they respect their husbands' decisions, and they keep quiet.

My mother is angry. This is her rage, the eruption of her rebellion against silence, but it is also the compendium of rage of her mother, her grandmother, and her great-grandmother, a rage which they themselves have not admitted possessing through twenty, thirty, who knows how many generations of submissive women.

"This anger," my mother says, her eyes reddened with fury, "is yours too."

My grandmother, with widened eyes and compressed lips, observes the bottom of her empty cup.

"And who perpetuates women's misery?" my mother asks. "Women themselves. The same women who never question the order of things and who educate their sons to be arrogant and their daughters to be servile."

She says this with a voice that is thick with so many harsh words. It is at once an affirmation and a challenge. Standing in the middle of the living room, she waits for a reply.

"You didn't educate me to be servile," my mother repeats, as she turns around to ask for an answer, a refutation, an admission, perhaps an apology.

My grandmother continues staring into her teacup.

What can she reply? Now, as I remember her gazing into that empty cup, I realize that she has no words with which to answer. I think that she fails to understand completely. My mother uses broad terms: history, generations. She speaks of women as a gender. My grandmother, on the other hand, adheres to the immediate: personal things, personal histories, but not History. She concerns herself with the future of her own children, with those faces that are familiar to her. My mother rises above all this: she ascends from the particular to the generic, and judges from up there.

My grandmother simply doesn't judge.

She, the grandmother who on her wedding day circled her groom in silence seven times as a sign of subordination, has renounced all options. During those seven turns, time regressed to the moment when Eve, holding the fruit of the Tree of Knowledge of Good and Evil in her hand, didn't bite into it, but rather handed it over, intact, to Adam.

"All right, then," my mother says, and falls onto the sofa. Her eyes are flooded with tears.

She moves to the armchair next to my grandmother and rests her head on my *bubbeh*'s shoulder. "All right," she says again, her eye makeup blurred by her tears.

"But your husband's father," my grandmother explains, as if trying to vindicate herself, "was a Biblical scribe." She lifts her hand to the nape of her neck to adjust her bun.

"Yes," my mother agrees, "the Bibles he wrote were rather famous."

I believe this encounter took place months after the one when my mother exploded with anger. On this occasion they're speaking Spanish because my mother wants the conversation to be for my benefit. "I want her to understand that the adult world isn't something that takes place behind closed doors or in secret languages."

My grandmother corrects her: "No, he didn't write Bibles. There is only one Bible, and it was dictated by God to the holy men of Jerusalem thousands of years ago."

"Well, then, he copied Bibles," my mother says. She takes a sip of Slivovitz. Yes: they are drinking a dark liquor from thimble-sized cups.

"No, that would be a sin, to copy the Bible," my grandmother says. "It would be falsifying it, something like that. Like saying God's name in vain, or blaspheming. He used to get up at dawn, pray, sit down before the scrolls, prepare the ink, sharpen the goose-quill pen,...Because I saw another scribe at work, the scribe of Krakow. And he would write the letters with *understanding*."

"Understanding?"

My grandmother gets tangled up in her words. I suppose that they switch languages a few times, and finally my grandmother makes herself understood. In any case, it is my mother who calls me over to explain it to me.

Understanding the value of each letter, because Hebrew letters, you know, are also numbers. Understanding the sum that each word represents. Hearing its sound. Understanding its meaning. Understanding why one word follows another, and how together they tell a story, and how the numbers in that story have certain connections to one another, certain delicate relationships.

"It was very slow work," my grandmother says. "Very slow. Very holy. Think of Einstein writing his formulas, that's how slowly your father-in-law must have worked. Before he could write it in the scrolls, he had to wait until each word would fill with light in his thoughts, like a revelation or a prophecy..."

My grandmother thinks it over for a moment and repeats: "Yes, a revelation or a prophecy."

"If only Gabriel would have inherited that patience," my mother remarks.

"But your husband became a communist."

"That has nothing to do with it," my mother says brusquely.

"It has everything to do with it. He became an atheist and a communist."

"Nothing to do with it," my mother insists.

My grandmother remains silent and allows my mother to calm down, just as she would allow a pudding to cool off. She says: "He cut his tie with God, and patience comes from God."

My mother lowers her gaze; perhaps she's thinking it over. Then she says, very quietly: "What can you expect from someone who breaks off from his own father? Betrayal, that's all."

"The good thing is that you can never break off from your parents," my grandmother says, raising the little glass to her lips. "The good thing," she continues, lowering the thimble-sized transparent crystal, "is that although someone may think that he has broken away from his parents, there is still something, *eppes vos geht*, that still continues."

"Very true," agrees my mother, nodding gravely. "Unfortunately there is always the subconscious."

My grandmother furrows her brow. Obviously her own daughter broke away from her at some given moment.

"Do you know why your son wants to be a mathematician?" my grandmother asks suddenly, her black eyes shining. "Because of your father-in-law, the scribe. For him, everything, from a flower to the stars, was numbers."

"My son knows nothing about my father-in-law," says my mother. "My father-in-law died in the war, and Gabriel never talks about him. You can't inherit traits from someone you never knew."

"I tell you, you can. The secret river that runs between generations comes from far in the past and continues on for a long distance. I have Sephardic features, but my mother didn't, and neither did my grandmother. Someone left Turkey for Poland a long time ago with this nose that she inherited from someone who came to Turkey from Spain during the time of Maimonides. Who knows how many generations of grandchildren and great-grandchildren come and go with straight noses, and suddenly there it is: my nose."

My mother looks up at the ceiling and tightens her lips, as though she were going to whistle. I promise myself never to forget this: the history of *Bubbeh*'s nose.

"And Sabita," my grandmother continues. "Sabita wants to be a writer. And it's also because of her grandfather, the scribe, although she never knew him, either."

"Please," my mother interrupts, sarcastically. "Did you know that Sabita gets thrown out of school at least three times a month? When she brings me a report card without red marks, maybe then I'll believe she wants to be something."

A long, painful silence follows. "To be some-thing," or rather, "to be Something," means (and even my grandmother understands this) to be something other than a woman, a housewife, a wife, a grandmother. It means to be a lawyer, for example, or a doctor, or a psy-choanalyst. What gives my grandmother the authority to argue with my mother, a university graduate? She leans over to serve herself more liquor in the thimble-glass. Since I may not argue with My Mother the Doctor, ei-ther, I allow myself to be defeated by her once again. Seated on the sofa, I slip down to the rug, where I lie on my stomach.

"But," adds my mother, trying to be conciliatory, "she might turn out to be a good athlete. She's a good swim-mer. She's on the club team."

Another long, painful silence. My grandmother holds up the liquor before her eyes and takes a sip.

"Jorgito, on the other hand," my grandmother adds in her usual measured way, "that one's going to be rich. It doesn't matter what he studies, because he'll always have money. He has my father-in-law's genes, and your mother-in-law's."

"You think he'll make money?" my mother asks, suddenly hopeful.

"Of course. Your mother-in-law is a very fine busi-nesswoman. She has the biggest store in town, and she sup-ported her husband, the Biblical scholar. Just like my fa-ther, who lived like an English lord in Galizia, always with his walking stick and a pearl stickpin in his tie, only even better than an English lord because he was touched by an-gels. Every gold coin he held in his hands multiplied into ten."

Behind them, through the lace curtains that cover the picture window, an intense, amber light is shining. Lying face down on the rug, I half-close my eyes. I see them as silhouettes, black shadows. Like a photo negative.

From that moment on, I keep doing it: half-closing my eyes. I see; I am absorbed in what I see. I know that no one has seen what I am seeing, that this is a singular moment. Although I cannot express all these feelings, I delight in the understanding—beyond words—and I savor the knowledge that I will remember this moment forever. There is something like a clean ribbon inside me where an absolute purity is being inscribed: the mind, my mother would say. *Ayn sof*, the substance of God, my grandmother would call it. *That*, as I have already named it: a ribbon of light where this moment is being recorded, where events that I perhaps do not yet understand are being inscribed, but which will come back to me to explain yet other events, that in turn will be explained, thanks to this memory. I am in love with my mind, with the substance of God, with *That*. Two shadows flutter in the curtains: two doves, behind my mother's and my grandmother's backs, and they alight on the railing of the terrace. I sigh deeply, again and again.

They continue talking about those strange phenomena: grandchildren who carry their grandparents within them. Now they're arguing about my uncle's children and my aunt's children. Sometimes, against the curtain, there is a quick flurrying of fleeting shadows, doves that come and go.

It gradually grows dark, or perhaps I am just falling asleep.

She blesses the *Shabbat* candles: her short, thin hands fly above the flames in very slow circles, six flames, eight flames, a crown of light circling the eight-branched silver candelabrum. A white lace veil on her head covers her eyes, as her lips murmur the prayer that welcomes and gives thanks for the Sabbath: the queen of the day of rest. The table is set for fifteen people: white plates with a cobalt blue border, cups, glasses, pitchers, my grandfather's silver glass at the head of the table. In the kitchen the food has been ready since nightfall. She has worked since the morning of the previous day, preparing the pickled herring, the carp, *gefilte* fish, stuffed fish, soup, noodles for the soup, the roast chicken, the pot roast, carrots with raisins, stuffed cabbage, fruit compote, strudel, apple pie, *challah*. Finally, when the sky turns coppery outside the living room window, she goes into the bathroom and removes the clothes that are redolent of seasonings and brine, and she bathes in the tub. She meticulously perfumes, combs and dresses herself. She paints her lips bright red before the vanity mirror. She puts on her gray pearl necklace and contemplates her appearance in the mirror: her black eyes, her gray pearl earrings, her navy raw silk dress. Preparing the food and preparing herself: she has done both with equal devotion. She has been accumulating the rituals that surround this day, that separate it from the rest of the week.

She has consecrated its hours, dissolving them into another time that is free from worldly pressures, a time that is charged with eternity. Between performing the duties of the ritual, she has served my grandfather his cup or two of tea; she has served dinner, and later, breakfast. She has come running when she heard his cries, like a man drowning behind his newspaper, and has snatched it away from him because he has been sinking in the morass of bad news. She has served him yet another cup of tea, mint this time, with four additional lumps of sugar, while he opened his copy of Maimonides's *Guide*, his tablet of salvation. At some point she opens the door for me, her youngest granddaughter; the elevator door opens up and she takes my little suitcase with my holiday clothes from my hand. She leans over to let me kiss her and throw my arms around her neck. She sits me down at the desk in the study so I can do my homework. She takes the two *challah*s from the oven. She hands my grandfather the wine-red velvet case that holds his prayer book, and she takes leave of him at the door. She goes from room to room, turning on the ceiling lights and the lamps, because once *Shabbat* begins, all work is forbidden, even the trivial task of turning on the lights. She disconnects the phone in the study: not even animals are allowed to work on *Shabbat*, so why should the telephone? she once explained to me, years before. She is bathed, dressed, and adorned. Then she calls me over to check my appearance: my Prince Valiant hairstyle, my cream-colored suit with a blue border on the collar and sleeves, my white socks neatly doubled over at the ankle showing through my dainty, transparent little plastic boots. She seems fascinated by my boots: she's never seen anything like them before, she says. "They're incredible," she says with astonishment. On the toes they have an iridescent pink plastic rhombus. "They're the latest thing," I explain.

When the point of light of the first evening star appears in the still-daylit sky through the living room window, we go to the living room, where she places the lace veil over her head and shoulders, lights the flames of the candelabrum and blesses them.

Smiling, she removes the veil. She takes me by both hands, moving her head from side to side. She moves her head to the slow rhythm of a secret music, the same rhythm that she marks with her feet. I imitate her. We move very slowly like this across the room. For one person or two to dance like this, alone, without music, is like offering flowers up to happiness. She bends over to whisper to me: "Feel *Shabbas* coming in, coming in…" She places the pads of her fingers on my heart. "Yes, that's where you feel it, that softness, coming in, coming in…*Es is lichtik*? Is it shining?" She passes her fingers across my eyelids, closing them.

Suddenly I notice a gesture of impatience or urgency in my grandmother. It's as though she wants to see inside me, to find out if her voice has reached me, if I share that light with her.

"Yes," I whisper, "I feel it."

We keep moving, slowly. "*Oyb es is lichtik, es is shayn*," she says. If it's shining, it's beautiful. "*Oyb es is shayn es is haylik*." "If it's beautiful," she whispers, "it's holy." She asks me in a breath of a voice if I understand. I, too, find it hard to speak, not to submit completely to that enchanted silence. I tell her *yes*, as if confiding a secret, *yes*, I understand. We're still moving, slowly. She says *no*, I don't understand yet. I should remember: it's beautiful, it's sacred. She hardly speaks, and when she does, she lacks the words for long explanations, so she uses aphorisms. Again she shakes her head, no, without stopping the dance. No, not now; it's not possible for me to understand it now, but I must learn it by rote: beautiful, sacred.

The neighborhood of Mexico City known as Hipódromo was built in the thirties where a race track once stood. The horse track became Amsterdam Avenue with its central promenade bordered by poplars which, during the time I'm now recalling, were ancient trees with majestic branches. And along Amsterdam and the nearby streets there were—now there are far fewer—many synagogues. On the afternoons preceding religious holidays, one would walk along the promenade and get the impression that this was a city with a flourishing Jewish quarter. One would encounter the ultra-Orthodox Jews in their black cassocks and long beards, their round-brimmed hats, prayer books tucked under their arms; their sons with *payes*, or long sideburns, falling in fringes; and their wives, whose shaved heads were covered with obvious wigs, would wear dark, ankle-length dresses with long sleeves and high necklines. One would also see Jews in modern, although still modest, attire: their heads covered with stylish hats or *yarmulkes*, little discs of black or white cloth. There were Jews in jeans, young people, with long, modish hairstyles, also wearing *yarmulkes*. The women wore tight-fitting miniskirts. Both sexes sported the blue shirts that were the emblem of the leftist, Zionist organizations.

My grandmother and I had to walk three blocks in order to reach Amsterdam Avenue, where we would adopt a slower pace. She would nod greetings to the people who passed by: friends, the children of friends, the grandchildren of friends.

I remember that particular *Shabbat*, that walk to the temple at my grandmother's side. I was wearing my transparent plastic boots. There was nothing unusual about that walk, except my little boots. Maybe my beige, imitation-leather cap. Or perhaps my plastic coat covered with iridescent green and pink rhombuses that matched the iridescent pink rhombuses on the toes of my boots and harmonized with my translucent plastic hoop earrings. Holding my grandmother's gloved hand, I was very much aware of my own elegance, and I pretended not to notice the glances that were cast in my direction. My uneasiness about being the center of attraction turned into a sort of self-conscious *hauteur*.

We arrive at the entrance to my grandparents' temple. There we meet four ladies, all wearing white gloves like my grandmother. They converse for a while in Yiddish. To me, it seems like a high society soirée: they represent old-style elegance, while I am elegance in its newest, most daring manifestation. They say something about a little Christmas tree, although I don't understand why, and they laugh. I check my hoop earrings; they're still there. And I laugh along with them, without knowing the reason why, but with delicate, distinguished laughter like theirs.

At a certain moment, the street lights switch on. In the center of the evening, my entire being—cap, plastic earrings, plastic coat, little plastic boots—is illuminated.

It's delicate, like picking a flower, or breaking a promise. I walk along holding her gloved hand, dressed in white. I'm wearing white jeans and tennis shoes with a gray sweatshirt and my hair is loose around my shoulders. At the end of the block, I see my girlfriends, also in jeans, tennis shoes, sweatshirts, wild hair. They haven't seen me yet holding my grandmother's hand. I don't want them to see her, my grandmother. It would be like their discovering that I'm still a little girl. With my friends I smoke little brown cigarettes; we crimp our hair, and we sing songs about unrequited love, and Beatles songs, in English. We paint each other's lips with flag-red lipstick. We talk about the variety of kisses that we might exchange with our boyfriends. That is to say, we're wild, we're daring. I exhibit my school expulsion notices to these friends like war medals, and family squabbles are ridiculous anecdotes that we exchange, howling with laughter. Perhaps they suppose, as I myself do, that, despite appearances, I am no longer a little girl. It's as though my grandmother were my discarded childhood, an old dress that they mustn't see. A tacky doll. I turn around: how tiny my grandmother is. I hardly have to raise my head to look into her eyes.

"I can go by myself," I tell her. "Go away."

She doesn't stop looking at me. But something has already happened: something subtle, like plucking a daisy.

I puff out my chest.

"Please," I beg.

She lifts her chin, looking up at the cloudy sky. I may be adding this detail to my memory. She presses her lips together, placing her gloved hand against my shoulder.

My God, that gloved hand, completely out of date.

I withdraw from her touch and run to the end of the block.

Now where does this deck of cards, this image, fit in? Before or after that incident? Before, I suppose, because I am clutching my grandmother's gray linen skirt, and I barely come up to her waist. She's looking for money for a taxi, groping around in her handbag, her eyebrows arched. She doesn't have enough.

We get on the bus; it's packed. Bricklayers coming home from work, servant girls in *huaraches*, plastic shoes, men in faded suits. She stands on the tips of her toes, but still can't reach the overhead bar. When the bus takes off, she trips backwards with me following, clutching her skirt. We fall on top of the people at the back of the bus. Her little hat is askew, her lipstick smudged. I snicker. She looks like a clown. I'm dying of laughter.

Some people get up to give us their seats in the back. My grandmother readjusts her pearl necklace, so that the largest pearls are in front. She arranges it with the greatest care. She's sitting very erect, smiling slightly at a gentleman with a cap and a skinny mustache who is avidly contemplating her: the most elegant woman in the world, with her smeared mouth and her crooked hat, its veil over one ear.

I don't say anything to her, but keep my lips tightly together to keep my laughter from escaping.

It's the Day of Atonement. God opens His book to inscribe some people for another year of life, but not the impious. There is still time today to recognize our sins and ask for forgiveness. It's a kind of bargaining with God: if one dares touch the root of his sins and repent, God will absolve him, but if one asks for forgiveness without touching the root of his sinfulness, God will ignore him.

My mother has sent me to ask for forgiveness along with my grandmother. She showed up in the synagogue at noon and sat for a half hour in the last row of the women's section. Most of the women were reading prayer books, but my mother sat among them absorbed in a different book: Freud's *The Interpretation of Dreams*. At this hour she was supposed to be in a classroom in the psychology department of the university, as part of her doctoral program. My father had to go to Acapulco on a business trip, at least that's what he said, but he promised he would fast.

I am twelve years old: for the first time in my life I'm expected to complete the twenty-four hour fast, without even drinking water. Even a sip would condemn me. For the first time, I am responsible for my actions and my misdeeds before God. I take it calmly. I couldn't possibly take it any other way, since I'm weak from hunger.

Then the dilemma presents itself. I climb the temple stairs very slowly. I have been playing charades with my friends on the Amsterdam promenade. In this leafy, vaulted promenade, children from the various synagogues get together to play. I climb the stairs very slowly. Leaning against the white walls, teenage couples converse quietly. I hear snippets of mundane conversations in romantic tones: "Then, will you come?"…"I like your…;" "Give me a…." I climb very slowly toward the chants to the King of the Universe and finally reach the landing.

On my left is the women's section. They pray seated, squeezed together. They pray muttering, or in silence, their lips compressed. They wear tennis shoes, to avoid the leather shoes that would be improper on this holy day. I watch the first row of benches, their heads covered with veils. They are seated near leaded windows that obscure their view. I observe the row of skirts, stocking-clad ankles, the row of tennis shoes on the floor, one after another, as in a shoe store display, some tennis shoes moving slightly, keeping rhythm with the prayers. I look up: some of the women are crying silently. My grandmother prays with her eyebrows arched, as though in a state of bewilderment. They're reading off the list of potential sins, so that everyone can settle accounts with God. Sins of deed, of thought, of petty emotions, of blindness to circumstance, of ignorance. A long catalogue of sins, five or six pages, that my grandmother reads with her arched eyebrows, surprised that so much evil could exist.

On my right is the men's section, much larger and more dramatic. They pray sitting or standing, rocking their torsos that are draped with white, blue-bordered shawls. They pray out loud, with throaty voices. Now they are chanting to God for forgiveness because we have sinned due to our wickedness or our limited capacity as human beings. This is how they express themselves: with the plural *we*. It's not enough for us to atone for our individuals sins, no: we Jews must atone for the sins of the entire world. Suddenly, all the men stand up and beat their chests with closed fists; they howl their pain, their remorse, their human limitations. My grandfather is the *chazan*, the cantor, during these grand ceremonies. He is standing on the central podium dressed in a white robe with a white shawl draped over his shoulders. He sings like an operatic tenor. His voice, dense and melodious, unfolds in arabesques, now spiraling in long flames to the heavens, now drowning in frightening groans, only to unfold once again.

Anguished and trembling, the men take their seats once more. But a few remain standing, rocking their torsos and pummeling their chests. These are the most perverse or the most devout: impossible to tell the difference.

I observe the men's tennis shoes. There's something so sporty about the Day of Atonement: those tennis shoes. Next to the rear window, a man in sky blue tennis shoes beats his chest with remarkable self-pity. Behind him, a group of children imitate him, each one shaking his body in a different direction. My brothers, behind them, fan their reddened faces to get some air. For the time being, the blows are over. Jorge isn't wearing a jacket, and his shirt, unbuttoned at the neck, is sticking out of his pants, his tie wrapped around his right wrist. Exhausted, he dries his sweaty forehead with his prayer shawl.

I know that this is a real decision. In previous years, I've walked into the men's section, loudly and animatedly, following a pure and innocent inclination. Now I am responsible for my actions. God is watching me. My actions will be inscribed in the Book.

My grandmother is also watching me, and she indicates with a gesture that I should come to her. I ignore her and go into the men's section. I climb up to the podium with my grandfather, hiding beneath his silk prayer shawl. That's it: I have chosen. I have very short hair and big eyes. I swim two kilometers every afternoon; my body is tense and erect. They throw me out of school for answering back. I will never again return to the section of mute women, even if God's own lightning strikes me.

Beneath my grandfather's silk shawl, I wait for the bolt of lightning to split me apart.

When twilight paints the treetops orange outside the rear window, a grave silence descends upon the temple. A man, covered with his white shawl, approaches the Ark of the Torah. He lifts the *shofar*, the ram's horn, to his lips. He blows into it, and the horn sounds. First there is a falling tone, then a tense, longer one. Something in the air changes: it grows thinner, it fills with new light; then the light grows brighter. The doors of heaven open up; men light their faces...I, still under my grandfather's shawl, cover my head with both hands. A nut, cracking between the jaws of a nutcracker: God's lightning, cracking your head open. That's what it must feel like.

It's lucky that my grandfather has never been fully aware of my age, and even now he doesn't realize that I am responsible unto God. He keeps praying and swaying his torso. I am this strange little bump under his shawl, a face that peeks out between his elbow and his waist to check on the condition of the heavens outside the window and the condition of the roof over our heads, and then hides once again with a worried expression.

During the remainder of the service I insist on remaining hidden beneath my grandfather's shawl.

We're walking along the Amsterdam promenade on the way to my grandparents' house. I am walking between them. A few steps ahead, my two brothers are walking along, talking to one another. Without her high heels, clad in tennis shoes, my grandmother is already shorter than I. I regard her, glancing downward out of the corner of my eye. And from time to time, I raise my eyes toward the sky: not even a trace of lightning. Among the tall fronds of the poplars there are stars, and a waning moon...

On the Day of Atonement the following year, I go to a small temple, minimalist. It's only one room in a private home on Amsterdam Avenue. The group that used to gather there to pray was made up of members of a socialist organization that became radicalized, according to them. The socialists' version of the story was that it dissolved into eclecticism. A hippie group. I'm talking about the tail end of the sixties now. All this means very little to me—I hardly know them. I'm the youngest in the group, the mascot, and those topics (socialism, hippie anarchism) are still unimportant to me. There are fourteen of us, dressed in light colors, not a single tie in the bunch, only one hat. We all have long, flowing hair. Flowers decorate the entryway, gladiolas, I think. In a white porcelain pot, a bunch of tall gladiolas are mixed in with fragrant tuberoses.

It's one single room where all of us, men and women, pray together. We sing in gentle voices, intoning some liturgical passages in Spanish and skipping over others. Adjoining this room there is a patio where pigeons scurry around in the overgrowth; their cooing voices punctuate the silences between prayers.

We say *O Lord Our God*, or *Our Lady Goddess*, or we change the references from the Most High to the Absolute. The Oneness, Eternal Blessedness, *Ollin*

Yolitzli—each one of us chooses the name that designates, at least provisionally, the Name that has no name.

Eva consistently calls it *That*. Moisés, this gorgeous, gorgeous guy who knows that he's gorgeous, calls it *Myself*, or even *My Divine Self*, when he feels particularly holy. I, a tad less conceited, call it *That*, or at times *Ayn sof*. Susi, who has a Jewish mother and a Catholic father, sometimes is bold enough to call it *Dear Virgin Mary* in a tiny voice, and then she glances around to took at the others, paranoia in her eyes. Pepe alternates between *Baruch Hashem* or Holy Spirit or *Ayn sof* or Tao or *Ollin Yolitzli*, leaping ecstatically from culture to culture in his melodic, clear voice. Our intention is to find the name or names that will resound in our hearts with the subtle impact of truth.

It's a bit chaotic, insouciant, this cluster of voices that rises up to God, blooming in twenty different directions and in as many different tones. It's free and light. Sometimes laughter, a quiet laughter, overtakes us. There's no cantor or rabbi to lead us. Our leader, whose authority is sporadic at best, is some guy with a long face and a hooked nose, sporting shoulder-length hair and a Zapata mustache, and who seems to suffer from omniscience. I say *suffer* because he goes around with a tormented expression on his face, his mouth stuffed with wisdom, as if possessing the Truth were like being possessed by some tyrannical spirit. The rest of us, as I've said, are not so burdened by our pact with God. No matter if we're the laughingstock of our siblings and our parents, we feel secure within the rich tradition of Universalist Jews. How could we feel otherwise in the company of such prestigious personages as Jesus, Joseph Caro, Luria, Spinoza…According to Luria, a Cabbalist, the Torah allows for a multitude of interpretations and rereadings, if it is indeed a book of divine revelation from on high, and we have embarked upon the task of rereading it, uninfluenced by previous dogma.

The Torah, says Luria, is a diamond with innumerable facets, and each facet represents a road for a human being. It awaits him from time immemorial to guide him to the luminous center of its written word. Luria considers the Torah to be perfect. Thanks to some inspiration of unknown origin, we consider ourselves to be even more perfect. Our motto is: scripture can be living or dead. If it is living, it must change, just as all living things metamorphose according to circumstances. We say those prayers that we consider to be holy, and we avoid those we consider obsolete.

Feelings, emotions: we are the feelings generation. Emotions are the bridge between the divine and the profane, the invisible and the opaque. How you feel is what you are: pleasure is good, sacred; pain is horrid; and everything else is ideology, empty words, deceit.

We pray with half-closed eyes. That interior light, the presentiment of That, and its first manifestation. It is a manifestation free of anthropomorphic metaphors: we have unmasked *Ayn sof*. We do not ask forgiveness, for we are the Chosen of the Light. We do not ask forgiveness, but we bathe in that light, in that pleasure. We pronounce its names, the sonorous metaphors of that light, that pure pleasure whose silence hums around us. We pray, inebriated with our own purity and with the fragrance of the tuberoses.

At dusk Moisés's father enters our synagogue, grabs him by the arm and drags him outside. They cross the patio, trampling the pigeons, shouting at each other, struggling among the pigeons that scatter through the air. Moisés's red hair, his father's black tie, Moisés's enraged green eyes, his father's thick lenses. His father lashes out with a slap to his face; Moisés responds by slapping back; his father's glasses go flying, as he falls down on the grass. The pigeons escape from their patio enclosure to the sky. The father regards his son, perhaps for the first time in years, and sees that he is tall and strong with red curls that fall to his shoulders. Finally his father gets up, looks for his glasses in the grass, and leaves. Moisés, with his angelic face, returns to us.

This event will have dire consequences: our friend will be called before the community authorities and will be offered a one-way ticket to Hebrew University in Jerusalem. He will exchange his ticket for one to India, where he will continue studying the names of God. Eventually he'll reach Jerusalem, the holiest city of three religions: Islam, Christianity and Judaism. Some years later, on a hilltop in Jerusalem crowned with svelte cypress trees, he will establish the first Zen synagogue.

After the service I walk along the promenade on Amsterdam to my grandparents' temple. I wait a while, and then approach when I see them emerging, surrounded by other Orthodox Jews. There's movement in my grandfather's eyes—he spots me, but he lowers the brim of his hat and keeps on walking. My brothers wave to me, but they don't lose pace with Grandfather. I walk behind them with my grandmother.

I walk along, holding her arm. She doesn't speak. It could be that fasting has worn her out more than usual this year. I'm in boots, she in tennis shoes, a little bent over. If I look at her sideways, I have to lower my glance.

I walk squeezing her arm against my side in a maternal gesture. But there's a certain pretense to my warmth, a certain barely-concealed arrogance. I'm playing at being my grandmother's mother.

She's tired. She's not wearing a hat, but rather a black lace veil on her head. She's not wearing gloves, either: she's finally realized that no one wears gloves anymore in this city. She walks along looking at the ochre-colored dust in the road, bent over, as I said.

She withdraws her arm to take my hand in hers. Her small, sinewy hand, with its tiny, delicate bones, like a bird's, I think.

She whispers: "Your grandfather thinks you didn't go to any temple. It's better that way. Your grandfather is sick," she says, "he shouldn't get upset."

I squeeze her hand a little. I'm waiting for her question: Why did you leave me today, on *Yom Kippur*?

The sound of steps in the dust, muted steps at my side: my grandmother in her tennis shoes. For an instant I feel ashamed of my loud footsteps.

She says, "Your mother mentioned something about pictures."

"I'm going to take some pictures," I say.

"There used to be a trolley here," she says. "Do you remember the Aizbergs? We used to go visit them on the trolley that went along Amsterdam."

I don't say anything, but the trolley ran along Insurgentes, five blocks away.

"Yellow," she says, smiling. "The trolley was yellow. Now I take a taxi to see the Aizbergs. Do you remember them?"

I tell her I hardly remember. Then we walk along in silence.

When we enter the lobby of the building, my grandfather is holding the elevator door open and my brothers move back, to give us room to come in. As soon as my grandmother goes in, my grandfather lets go of the door.

I take the stairs up.

It's curious: my mother and her brother announced that Grandfather wouldn't last another year, and they want to have pictures of his last *Yom Kippur*. They should know, they're attentive to their parents' health. All I know is that my grandfather takes medicine with nitroglycerin, and that the atom bomb, it seems to me, also contains nitroglycerin, so I'm careful not to upset him, to make sure he doesn't have to move too much when I pose him for the photos.

The pictures must be scattered among the houses of my closest relatives now: my uncle's house, my cousins', lost among long-expired postcards and other detritus: nostalgia is not a virtue in our family. Black and white, clumsy photographs. My grandfather at the head of the table, slicing the *challah*. My grandfather with his children by his side. The picture with the football-team arrangement of old people and teenagers and children, the entire family with grandfather at the center, without ever having moved from the head of the table. Here and there my grandmother's image appears, smiling.

Behind the resplendent, half-filled wine glasses, the pitchers and empty bottles, beneath the unfocused glare of the huge crystal chandelier, the tall flames and the melted-down candles, the Great Patriarch: his thick lips ironed flat by centuries of tedium.

My grandmother, alone. No such photo exists. When I try to imagine her that way, the image rings false even in my imagination.

My grandmother with her first great-grandchild, Fay, standing in her lap, her arms half-extended, each little hand clutching one of my grandmother's hands, the astonished expression of an unwilling acrobat. Hilda, the baby's mother, standing a step behind them.

My grandmother and my mother, sitting on a black bench. My mother has a bouffant hairdo, a dark-blonde helmet. She's looking ahead, towards a corner of the room, not at the camera. She's already showing some pronounced lines between her brows, two vertical lines that extend toward her forehead. Her expression of authority, of obstinacy in the face of circumstances, have now become her actual face. Her arm encircles my grandmother's shoulder, but only her hand is actually touching *Bubbeh*'s shoulder, gingerly. My grandmother looks straight at the camera, smiling with amusement. It amuses her to watch me being a photographer. She hasn't forgotten about me in choosing a portrait of herself: her gray hair, interspersed with white locks, is pulled back in a bun. She's not sitting straight; I think, she's tired. Irreparably tired, tired by my grandfather's illness. Yet in that oval frame, completely marked by wrinkles, her eyes—her eyes are still fresh, still alive.

My grandfather no longer goes to the brush factory; he's fed up, he says. The world doesn't work right,
he's said that for a long time now. People are ungrateful,
especially when they join unions and go on strike. But if
he hates people, it's purely objective on his part. "If I eat
honey," he says, "it tastes sweet; if I eat salt, it's salty. If I
consider humanity,..." and here he makes a horrible face
and sticks out his tongue. The human condition is abhor-
rent: we Jews are not the only ones who are in eternal exile
from our homeland. Each human being is a wandering soul
in exile; the world, the entire universe, is our exile.

"Those who were never born are the lucky ones,"
he says, and smiles a melancholy smile. "Unfortunately,"
he adds, "there aren't too many of them." He never says: I
don't feel good. He never says: this hypertension is terrible. We all know that he's ill; the electrocardiogram graphs
that document his discomfort lie on my mother's night table.
Next to them, there is an envelope containing a strange bit
of black mica: the X ray of his heart. It's a black mass with
a little white spot, a little stone in his left ventricle.

Although his hatred is ecumenical, my grandfather
is still capable of establishing his preferences: he hates Che
Guevara above all other human beings. He hates his sol-
dier-of-fortune spirit: what's that hick doing liberating foreign countries and encouraging starving peasants to think

about forming their own utopia? If he happens to see Che's picture in the newspaper, he slams his fist down on top of it. Strange, since Fidel Castro, widely considered to be Che's spiritual brother in those days, seems admirable to him: "He's like Herzl, the founder of Zionism." Ah, a Sephardic prince, that Fidel. Pope John XXIII inspires him to fold his hands piously over the paper: a *tzadik*, he says, a wise man. The Pope has exonerated all the Jews of the crucifixion of the Son of God, and my grandfather is grateful to him, but he still needs to discuss the matter of whether any individual can be the Son of God more than anyone else, and besides, whose God? Any photo of Díaz Ordaz, the president of Mexico, unfailingly receives a blow of his fist. "Nazi crook," he says, snorting with anger. The increasingly frequent shots of students with placards protesting the government make him shake his head sadly. He leans over the photo and speaks quietly to the students: "Study," he tells the faces in the photo, "study medicine, engineering. Make bandages, make bridges, you fools."

He doesn't read the paper, he has no patience for it. He browses through it, looks at the photos, punches them, talks to them, shreds up the paper, and squashes the pieces into a ball. Next my grandmother serves him a cup of tea with four lumps of sugar and four drops of sedative, and then he opens Maimonides's *Guide for the Perplexed* and calms down for a half-hour, an hour or even two.

Later, his anguish returns, and he ambles around the apartment, looking for something to do, while my grandmother tries to keep him from having another one of those attacks of fury that make him break out in cold sweats and get dizzy. The nitroglycerin pills at noon are a miracle: they put him to sleep. He wakes up calmer. It's the passage of time that irritates him: the messenger arriving from the market with notices of overdue bills, a postcard from my brother at Boston University. ("Mathematics? Why does he need to study mathematics? Isn't medicine good enough for him?") The ace of hearts appearing in the middle of his game of solitaire in the study makes him curse like a condemned man.

In September of 1968 my grandfather cancels his subscription to the newspaper. To keep abreast of events happening in this accursed world he relies on the nightly television broadcast. Sitting in the study in his green corduroy armchair, he watches television, occasionally muttering, *tzeshisen*, shoot. On average every night he sends five politicians and three actors straight to hell.

He's condemned Elvira Quintana to the inferno on countless occasions. It so happens that right before the news, the soap opera *The Pain of Loving* comes on, starring this actress. A beautiful orphan girl who works in a flower shop seduces a married man, who plays Chinese checkers with her every afternoon and gives her money, ostensibly to support and educate her five younger siblings (who don't really exist), while in their palatial mansion, the gentleman's wife and two children cry continually, destroying each other with bitter recriminations. My grandfather plays his game of solitaire in the study, and while he methodically shuffles the deck, he comments to himself about the melodramatic episodes. His only comment: *tzeshisen*.

Sometimes he turns off the television and plays solitaire in silence. He unbuttons the collar of his white shirt, ceremoniously rolls up the sleeves, and lights up a Raleigh. Recently, he's started smoking.

It's always the same hierarchy: the jack, the queen, ten, nine, eight, all the way down to the ace. Columns of cards, aligned in parallel rows, covering the glass that protects the wooden desk top. He bends over the cards, putting them in sequence according to an inflexible law, putting in order that which chance has created.

The game is over: the desired order has been achieved. But there is still an unanswered question.

He gathers up the cards in two stacks, revealing the images that are now visible between the glass and the wooden desk top. A photo of my grandfather as a young sergeant in the Polish Army, with his handlebar mustache, a whip in his right hand, his boots, the black steed's bridle in his grip. A postcard with frayed edges: the brush factory in Bielsko-Biala. An oval passport photo, the round edge of the seal biting off half the face of the prematurely aged man who was my grandfather at age forty-six, some twenty years ago. A drawing of a rabbi in a striped robe, leaning over the open scrolls of the Torah. And my grandmother with her first great-granddaughter, Fay, standing in her lap, as Hilda, her granddaughter, stands behind them.

Although I don't know for sure, I suppose that he can't quite manage to put those five or six images of the deck in order. He doesn't manage to arrange them in a way that gives him peace. The chronology in and of itself has only trivial meaning. And to admit chance as the decisive factor in his life would be unthinkable: it would be like imagining a God who shakes His creatures like dice in the palm of His hand.

He shuffles the two stacks several times. He plays another game of solitaire. He places one pile face down, the other with the numbers face up. One is a secret, the other a revelation. One stack, then another. He begins to reorganize and readjust what has been shuffled. Or he goes into the living room to attend to that other solitary pursuit, the *Guide for the Perplexed*. Maimonides adjusts human experiences according to their proximity to the Absolute, according to the ancient law of Moses.

But at eight o'clock he turns on the television set again and settles into his armchair to carry on a conversation with the most powerful people on the planet. "Yes, yes, I already know all that about Hitler," he tells Díaz Ordaz. "Order and national pride and blah-blah-blah, and you're the Fatherland and your enemies are Chaos personified. Antiochus Epiphanes said all that twenty centuries ago, so let me do you a favor," he says, as he raises his right hand and lets it fall again. *"Tzeshisen,"* he says.

In October military tanks roll down the street, olive green behemoths with six pairs of tires each. By noon their noise reverberates throughout the apartment, and inside the glass doors of the living room china cabinet, the porcelain cups shake. It's a sunny afternoon, but the air is cold; it rained this morning. In the back of the apartment, in his study, my grandfather sits on the corduroy sofa, wrapped in a goose down comforter, nursing a bad cold. His face is all swollen; he coughs. Since he arrived in Mexico twenty-five years ago, military mobilization has always gone on in far away places, in other latitudes.

Behind him, the picture window vibrates ceaselessly. At times it seems as though it's about to crack and shatter, especially whenever a helicopter passes overhead. He nestles into his comforter, cocooned in the malaise of his flu. At night he refuses to watch the news.

My grandmother listens to the radio as she prepares dinner and finds out about the student massacre in the plaza. There is talk of two hundred or two thousand young people riddled with bullets—everything is uncertain. She brings a basin filled with warm water into the study. She kneels down in front of my grandfather, removes his slippers and moves his feet toward the water. She washes his feet, wordlessly.

Finally, one morning it happens. My grandfather is reading the *Guide for the Perplexed*, immersed in the ultimate redoubt of his happiness, when he raises his eyes to the ceiling and calls my grandmother. He announces to her that Maimonides is useless too. "So much wasted intellect," he says.

"This Maimonides wrote for Greeks, after all, people who believed in logic. It's useless to try to penetrate Mystery with logic. Mystery is Mystery. There is nothing else to do with Mystery but to accept it. Blessed are the blessed, and that's that," he says. "The unlucky are simply unlucky, and that's all." Disconsolate, he closes the *Guide*. After a lifetime of studying it, it turns out that it's all in vain.

My grandmother, alarmed, calls my mother at her office. My mother doesn't know how to react: she also believes that the so-called *Guide* is a compendium of superstitions. My uncle visits my grandfather, and my grandfather tells him a parable. A frightening parable, according to my uncle.

He walks around the office of my mother's clinic, a fifteen-by-fifteen foot bare room, without any pictures, with a window overlooking a six lane highway, the miniature cars continually following a path from the upper frame of the window to the lower.

"Or don't you think it's a terrible parable?" my uncle asks.

Santiago, my mother's former analyst and her intellectual tutor, is seated on the divan. His mane of curly hair is now completely white. I'm sitting at his side. My mother sits in her black leather psychoanalyst's chair.

"It's because of the war," my mother says, finally.

My mother is discussing her father's life with the distant, dispassionate tone of an historian, as she crosses her legs and stares at a white wall. By the age of forty-five, my grandfather was one of the most powerful industrialists in Poland, the leader of the Jewish community in Bielsko-Biala, and his house was the meeting place for all the founding Jewish thinkers of that community. Vladimir Jabotinsky, the Zionist leader, relied on his financial and moral support. In the Glickman factory young people were trained to use industrial tools, while the Zionist organization planned their immigration to Israel. His house, similarly, was a place where famous rabbis would spend the night whenever business brought them to the area. My grandfather was especially devoted to Rabbi Gershom, a follower of Maimonides and therefore a proponent of the rationalist approach to studies of the Torah. He disapproved of the mystics and envisioned a Judaism that would be tied to Western scientific thought. And every month, when the Catholic prince of the province would sit down to dinner at his table, my grandfather would pin his World War I decoration onto his lapel in honor of the occasion. That gold medal had been conferred upon him for his services as administrator of the arsenal of the Polish Army. To speak with the prince about politics or business while displaying the medal on his lapel was to announce silently, but without false modesty: I am necessary. World War II removed my grandfather from the ranks of the important decision-makers forever.

"It turned him into a nobody," my mother murmurs.

My uncle sticks a cigarette into a short ebony holder and bites down on the mouthpiece, moving towards the window.

"And the worst of it is this," says my mother. "The war got into him here," she says, touching her forehead, "and here," placing two fingers against her heart.

I think about that white spot on the X ray of my grandfather's heart, the little pebble in his left ventricle. For a full minute, the only sound is that of the traffic fifteen stories below.

"For him," says Santiago, "the war never ended."

"Maybe you're right," my uncle says, pausing before the window. "Maybe it didn't end."

Santiago nods. "It didn't end," he agrees.

This is the parable of the idiot who wanted to illuminate the darkness. My grandfather relates it in a quiet voice as my uncle listens. They're sitting at a corner of the long dining room table, and my grandfather smokes between sentences, flicking the ashes into a little porcelain dish as he taps the cigarette with his index finger. At the other end of the table my grandmother slices the apple strudel that has recently come out of the oven.

An idiot was fascinated by the mystery of darkness, and he decided to discover what darkness was really like, to unearth its *mystery*. Taking a lantern, he stepped into the darkness. He lit the lantern and saw a tree. He said: "Aha! So, darkness is a tree." Then he moved the lantern and saw a white horse, standing there in the blackness of the night. "Aha!" he said, "then darkness is really a horse." He extinguished the lantern. How was it that darkness could descend upon his eyes if he already knew that it was something else, a tree or a horse? He lit the lantern again. The light swept over the darkness and illuminated a black hen. "Of course, of course, that's what it is—a black hen! That's what darkness is, without a doubt," he said enthusiastically, and quickly extinguishing the lantern, he swore never again to lose his faith. Then the idiot wrote a book about the three stages of understanding darkness.

We're riding in the gray Valiant, an old model, with my grandfather driving, my grandmother next to him, and with me in the back seat. We're clipping along at the amazing speed of thirty-five miles per hour around Mexico Park. It's a windy afternoon.

An aggressive busdriver comes up close behind us, tooting his horn. "*Oy-oy-oy*," my grandmother moans. Again, the busdriver hits the horn, but my grandfather doesn't speed up.

"Nazi," my grandfather utters.

"*Oy-vay*," my grandmother says, which is the same thing as *oy-oy-oy*.

"Speed up," I say. "Speed up or else park."

"Wait," replies my grandfather. "Wait ten years and you'll have your own car."

"One more year," I say. "You can get your license here at fifteen."

"So wait less," he grumbles. "I'll die and leave you this one."

He doesn't speed up, he doesn't park, and the busdriver honks relentlessly. My grandfather slows down even more and starts honking the Valiant's horn.

"Let me out!" I shout. My grandfather hits the brakes, and I climb out. I open the door on my grandmother's side. "Get out," I say.

I think my grandmother is confused, since she gets out of the car with a flustered expression. The bus sounds its horn once again, my grandfather pulls away, and we watch the Valiant round the corner and disappear.

"*Oy-oy-oy*," my grandmother repeats.

So tiny. In her pale gray silk dress that's a size too big for her. She's wearing medium heel shoes, and yet I'm a head taller than she.

It's a windy afternoon, and I take my grandmother by the elbow as we enter the park.

It is not in vain that memory is tidy. We walk through the trees being blown around by the wind. The sky is luminous, with clouds crossing quickly. My grandmother glances up to watch the fleeting clouds.

We sit down on an iron bench that surrounds a fountain. A subtle breeze reaches us from the spouting water off to one side. My grandmother tips her head, allowing the breeze to play with her hair. There's a halo of white hair surrounding her. Her face looks surprised, distended, bathed in the intensity of the afternoon.

She points to her ear with one finger. I understand: she wants me to listen to the sound of the wind in the branches. It's a sustained humming. The trembling park, the branches stretching toward the south, the forty-foot high, curving palm trees, their leafy fans whistling, and even higher, the ancient poplars, in pursuit of the escaping clouds—everything is radiant with sunshine.

My grandmother takes a deep breath.

"No one has ever seen the wind," she says in Yiddish. "We can see what it does, we can hear what it does, we know what it does, but no one, nobody, has ever seen the wind." This is what my grandmother says. She used to say the same thing about time: that no one has ever seen time. She closes her eyes as she speaks. She places two fingertips in the center of her chest.

I know that gesture. When she is overcome by emotion, she touches her chest lightly, as if to remember that she's there. I think about what she has just said, and I think that the idea is much more beautiful in Spanish. *Viento, tiempo*: the wind and time. I bring my head next to hers and whisper the Spanish words in her ear, a secret.

She sighs and extends her open hands. From the fountain, the breeze brings the scent of chlorophyll. My grandmother looks up again, her open hands still extended in front of her. Her mouth half-opens. I watch her with the same childlike curiosity with which she regards the clouds.

From between the tree trunks there are sudden visions: clouds of dry, yellow leaves that cross over, pile up, and tumble. We can hear the tinkling of an ice cream vendor's bell, although we can't see him. We can only hear the high-pitched bell.

I look up also. Some distant clouds, as tenuous as gauze, cross the horizon. And granules of light, nearly transparent, falling, falling. More subtle than the wind, this light descends vertically among the gusts, but the wind doesn't move it one bit.

A little boy runs toward us, suddenly turning and leaping towards the fountain. With a prodigious leap, he rises up into the wind and falls into the water. No, no, it's not a child—it's a big, brown paper bag sinking into the water.

My grandmother covers her face with her moist hands.

I slip between and among the adults. Someone is sobbing. Someone, my uncle, is crying. The cemetery attendant says that my grandmother died in the bathtub. She had even washed her hair; there was no need to wash the body, as prescribed by the burial rites. Her body lies on a plank. It's so small and spare, with no breasts, like the body of a young girl. Her skin is greenish. Her pubic hair is very black, just like her eyes behind her closed lids.

My mother glances around uneasily, to avoid looking at the body. My father hugs her shoulders, kisses her face, her tears. My mother wraps her arms around his waist and buries her head in his chest. My grandfather rubs his hands together, sobbing.

I resolve to look at the body, to overcome rejection or fear. But even when I conquer my fear, it doesn't diminish. Rather it grows and becomes voluptuous in its intensity, like the voluptuousness of illness or fever. I have a sense that the body is calling me. I reach out my hand, but it hangs in the air. Her pubis, the only part of her that seems alive, her black pubic hair. I can hardly resist the temptation to touch it. Death, I hadn't noticed it.

My grandfather gasps for air.

They wrap the body in a white sheet.

The children, the children's spouses, the grandchildren, the spouses of the older grandchildren, my grandfather's sister who has flown in from New York, my grandmother's three nephews who have arrived on the same flight, forty or fifty old people—the entire congregation of my grandparents' synagogue—old Mr. Aizberg and his wife, some middle-aged friends and younger relatives: we all follow the draped body behind the gravediggers who are carrying it.

Around the grave a rabbi speaks, a cantor sings, all against a background of silence that is interwoven with crying. Farther back, against the wall of the cemetery, outlined against the sky with its uniform white clouds, some blue cypresses.

They deposit the draped body down there into the tomb. Shovelsful of dirt begin to fall.

For whatever reason, my grandfather and I return to the apartment first. My grandfather, with his scowling face. We go in. He collapses into an armchair, takes off his hat and drops it on the rug. He gets up and heads for the back rooms. I watch him disappear behind the wooden screen that conceals the door frame.

He calls her: "Minke, Minke! Germinie!"

He calls out to her in Yiddish, Hebrew, Polish, German. In the study, in the parlor, in the bedroom. On the balcony, suspended five stories above the street. He returns to the kitchen and calls her: "Minke, Minke!"

Suddenly, he's quiet in the middle of the living room. He breathes heavily. Slowly, he fixes his eyes on mine, as if he didn't know me. He looks at me with the hard look you give a stranger you don't want anything to do with. He smacks his lips and mumbles: "Some tea."

I go to the kitchen to make him a cup of tea. Then I notice, hanging from the ceiling, the piece of gauze my grandmother used for draining her homemade cheese. On the stove, a pot of soup, fragrant with chicken and parsley; the casserole with sweetened carrots; the bowl of fruit compote. I open the refrigerator: it's full. The ceramic dish full of herring, another with carp; the *gefilte* fish; the jar of horseradish...inside the oven, already cooled, four loaves of *challah*.

She had prepared the *Shabbat* dinner. But those four *challahs* puzzle me: four. She always made two.

When I return to the living room with the tea-tray, my grandfather is in his shirtsleeves, seated at the head of the mahogany table. With his glasses riding the tip of his nose and his lips parted, he's reading the *Guide for the Perplexed*. I serve him the tea, and with the silver tongs, I deposit four lumps of sugar into his cup. I sit down near my grandfather, awaiting the outburst of indignation against the stupid ruse that Maimonides is using to try to console him.

He reads the first page of the text. For the first half hour, he reads the same page, expressionlessly. Then he turns his head to the side and looks at the right-hand corner of the Persian rug, his lips still parted.

I go to the bedroom to lie down on one of the twin beds. It's impossible: the mirror over the dresser stops me cold. Reflected in the mirror, I see the antique pearl necklace entangled in the silver handle of the hairbrush. Among the white bristles there is a long, white hair.

I lie face down on the cold parquet floor.

My mother stumbles across me. She opens the closet door and removes several white sheets. I feel her moving nearby. When she unfolds a sheet to drape it over the mirror, the room is filled with the sweetish scent of lavender. I think, I should get up and help cover the other mirrors in the house, according to the rituals for mourning, but I remain lying on the parquet.

There is that familiar mechanical sound, that clock: my heart.

She died on Friday morning. Since all human labor, including burial, is prohibited during *Shabbat* from Friday evening onward, we had to take care of all the funeral arrangements quickly and bury her around five o'clock in the afternoon.

The family is arriving, along with my grandmother's close friends and the best friends of her children. They arrive, take their seats, and keep quiet. The children and husband of the deceased sit on the floor, leaning against the wall. It's like a family party, only backwards. No one says hello when arriving, and no one speaks. Everyone breathes in the thick air of my grandmother's absence.

Timid and fearful, the Aizbergs arrive. They look so old and worn out, as sad now as when there was no death to mourn, I think to myself. I don't know, they seem to be wearing the same age-polished clothing as when I knew them before, in those days when I was no more than a child, just learning to walk. They sit down in two chairs in the corner—for five minutes, no longer.

Before they leave, Mr. Aizberg kneels down next to my uncle. He tells him in Yiddish that he's so sorry, so sorry, but nonetheless, they still depend on that gold coin that my grandmother gave them every month. Like a sleepwalker with puffy eyes, my uncle nods assent. On a little pink scrap of paper, a bus ticket, Mr. Aizberg writes down his address, and on another piece of paper, some telephone numbers: my uncle's, my grandparents' house, the business. Maybe so that he can call to remind him about the money.

My uncle takes the tickets and stares at them blankly. "Well," he says after a while, "these are mine, and this...Is this one your office address?"

Aizberg seems to understand that my uncle is distracted. "You bring money here," he says, "den ve know." And he repeats how much this hurts him: "So sorry, so sorry."

Then my grandfather, sitting next to my uncle, says he needs a Kleenex. With a tragic expression, he thrusts his head in Aizberg's direction, appealing to him directly. "There's some in the bathroom," he confides. Aizberg gets up and plods with his worn-out gait toward the bathroom, where my grandmother died in the tub. We all watch him as he approaches the door. He stands paralyzed in the doorway, his face dark.

He stands there for at least six minutes.

With the lights turned off, the bathroom must look black, and in the blackness the tub must look like a coffin.

Mrs. Aizberg waits in her chair, terrified, rubbing her hands together.

Mr. Aizberg returns and keeps on walking toward the front door, his frightened wife running feverishly behind him. For just one instant, my grandfather's grayish blue eyes seem to light up.

The men from the synagogue who will form the *minyan* for the *kaddish*, the prayer for the dead, begin to arrive. The living room is packed.

Their heads covered with white silk shawls, their bodies swaying, they pray, facing the oil painting of yellow sunflowers that hangs on the wooden wall. My grandfather's thick voice, straining with tautness amid the other prayers, cracks and tears from time to time.

Suddenly, through the picture window, the light of the first evening star twinkles in the still-daylit sky: *Shabbat* has begun and all sadness is forbidden by Holy Writ. A twenty-four hour interlude in the mourning period. The men from the synagogue take their leave, wishing everyone a holy and peaceful Shabbat. I remove the sheet from the mirror in the living room, and suddenly all the lamps in the room are multiplied. The women share the tasks: they add two wooden leaves to the table; they spread out the table-cloth; they set the table; they warm up the food.

Although the table is set, something is missing. I know where my grandmother kept her silver candlesticks, and I place them in the middle of the table. I light a candle, begin to utter the prayer over the *Shabbat* candles, and then stop.

"*Gut*, that's good," I hear my mother say. Leaning against the wall, she looks at me intently. Because of her age, she should be the one to light the candles, and after her, my grandmother's daughter-in-law. Then, my two female cousins.

"*Gut, mach dos*, do it."

I can't remember if my mother ever spoke to me in Yiddish before or after this occasion.

"*Ich hob fargessen die Brucha*," she says. Anyway, I've forgotten the prayer.

I light the wicks and pronounce the blessing while my hands pass over the flames. I cover my eyes.

We're seated around the long table, eating my grandmother's carp, her *challah*, her *gefilte* fish, the horse-radish, the pickled herring. My grandmother had prepared enough for the usual *Shabbat* crowd as well as for the family members who have come to her funeral. Next, we concentrate on the noodle soup, a golden broth with long, slippery noodles, made the previous afternoon. Then, the meat: the tender breast of chicken, the more resilient pot roast in gravy. We eat ravenously: white meat, red meat. The crystal bowls containing sweetened carrots or mashed potatoes or sliced cucumber salad with parsley and vinegar pass from hand to hand the length of the table. Bottles of Carmel wine, salt and pepper shakers, the jar of horseradish, bottles of seltzer: there's no end.

I look at the serene flames of the eight-branched candelabrum with wax running down its silver sides, the pitchers of cut crystal refracting the light. I look at that line of faces, chewing, bringing the white meat and red meat to their mouths. I notice those short, aquiline noses that several of us inherited from my grandmother, that nose transported from Maimonides's Golden Age Spain, through Greece, through Poland, to Mexico. My grandmother's black eyes, along with those noses, or different noses.

We are ingesting my *bubbeh*; she is already inside her grandchildren. How strange: grandparents inside their grandchildren. We drink red wine, scarlet, too much of it. Someone bites into a sour pickle and starts to laugh. A silence. But then the laughter is more frequent. Someone tells a joke. I'm laughing and feeling dizzy at the same time. Slowly, I chew the meat. I look at the gravy on the dish. It's reddish-brown, like old blood. On one side of the shiny, muscle-like slice of beef, that puddle of old blood. I raise a thin slice of beef to my mouth. Fighting my repugnance, I bite, chew, eat, swallow. My uncle stands up, places the palms of both hands on the table, and clears his throat.

He says solemnly: "We have left our first dead in this land."

He remains standing; I wonder if he expects applause.

He remains standing, in his black silk suit, his white silk shirt, and his black silk tie, cut off halfway down from the knot as a sign of mourning.

He remains standing while the overlapping conversations tentatively begin again. And we start to eat again, drinking, chewing, swallowing up my *bubbeh*.

I feel sick and lie down on the sofa. I fall asleep.

Later that night I sit down on the sofa with my mother and I tell her what I imagine my grandmother's final moments were like. My mother listens to me with parted lips, her eyes red from crying.

She tells me: "You have a morbid imagination. Do you know what *morbid* means?"

Before I can reply, she says: "You know what I'm talking about. At your age, you can understand. What you're saying is horrible, horrible."

"It's shiny," I say. I place the pads of two fingers, my ring finger and my index finger, on my heart as my grandmother used to do whenever something touched the innermost part of her being, whenever something opened her heart to that superhuman essence, without beginning or ending, that light, *Ayn sof.*

My mother sees the gesture, recognizes it. She knows what it means. She averts her glance. The gesture annoys her; coming from me, it irritates her. Like her, I too have given up trying to conserve my grandmother's religious rituals: I don't say the blessing over bread, I ride in a car on *Shabbat*, I answer the phone. Why, then, do I conserve my devotion to that light? It's obstinacy on my part, she's told me, intellectual impurity. Magical thinking, she would call it sometimes. When I would try to explain that I was talking about a light that is absolutely visible, both within me and without, and that it's not that I feel devotion *to* that light, but that the light itself *is* devotion, it's enough for me to look at it and feel grateful, not grateful towards anyone or anything in particular, not grateful for anything special, but simply grateful. Usually, my mother would already be moving away from the conversation. But this time she stays, sitting on the edge of the bed, looking at one corner of the ceiling.

"It's…, " I begin to say, but I can't catch my breath.

Finally I say it in a tiny thread of a voice, using my grandmother's words: "It's beautiful, it's sacred."

"Shiny," my mother whispers, "beautiful, sacred." She nods her head. "Sacred," she repeats, and she snorts. "And what about horror?"

"Horror too."

I can imagine her. She's finished her work in the kitchen. She's prepared a meal for twenty-five people or more, twice what she usually prepares. Perspiring, smelling of chicken soup, her hands redolent of garlic and fish, she goes into the bathroom, closes the door, turns on the light. She removes her apron, her dress, her stockings, underwear. She folds each garment carefully, placing them on the little pewter stand.

She turns on the faucet in the tub. She undoes her bun in front of the mirror over the washbasin. Her white hair, with a few gray locks.

She lowers herself into the tub, leans back, resting her head on the rim. Everything is white: white and transparent. The steam from the water rising up to the ceiling, the light bulb, so yellow that it appears white, the gleaming tiled walls, beaded with steam, the foggy mirror above the sink. Beneath the surface of the water, her tiny body, like that of a twelve-year-old girl, only softer, seemingly oscillating. The water makes her look even shorter than she is: a little dwarf-lady. The body of a nursing mother: tender, her translucent skin delicately wrinkled at the crevices.

She's finished her chores: each and every corner of the house is clean, each candlestick polished. Each child, each grandchild, is fully grown and delivered unto the world. Everything is impeccable in anticipation of *Shabbat*, the time beyond time. She sighs. The only touch of black that can be found is in her eyes and her black pubic hair. She closes her eyelids.

Behind her closed eyes, that light. Her conscience: *Ayn sof.*

In that light, perhaps, the words are forming: "*Baruch Ata Adonai, Eloheinu Melech Cholam*: Blessed Art Thou, Lord Our God, King of the Universe."

And then that white thought dissolves into blood.

I can imagine even more. Her body remains like that for a while, recumbent, the nape of her neck resting on the edge of the tub, veiled in steam. Then she stretches out more and more. And then some more. She begins to slip under the water. She slips to the bottom of the tub. She is there, lying beneath the water.